# Mint Freeze Murder

## A SPIES AND FOOD TRUCK COZY MYSTERY BOOK 2

### ROSIE A. POINT

Mint Freeze Murder

A Spies and Food Trucks Cozy Mystery Book 2

Cover by Fantasy Fig Designs

# You're invited!

Hi there, reader!

I'd like to formally invite you to join my awesome community of readers. We love to chat about cozy mysteries, cooking, and pets.

It's super fun because I get to share chapters from yet-to-be-released books, fun recipes, pictures, and do giveaways with the people who enjoy my stories the most.

So whether you're a new reader or you've been enjoying my stories for a while, you can catch up with other like-minded readers, and get lots of cool content by visiting my website at *www.rosiepointbooks.com* and signing up for my mailing list.

Or simply search for me on *www.bookbub.com* and follow me there.

I look forward to getting to know you better.

Let's get into the story!

Yours,
Rosie

# One

"Barkington, wait!" The cry came from Hentie, my co-server on the I Scream for Ice Cream truck, which was parked near the boardwalk that overlooked the bay.

My lips quirked at the corners.

Hentie, wearing a bubblegum blue pants suit and an apron, chased after her adorable Chihuahua, Barkington, who had a knack for getting into trouble and barking at anything that moved—or even things that didn't.

This morning, he'd taken particular offense to a bench and table with a quaint purple umbrella that overlooked the bay. Beautiful blue waters, free of that darn cruise ship, and the docks far below—the lobster boats had gone out long ago. Carmel Springs had a sliver of pale sandy beach, and a boardwalk that was packed with stores and restaurants.

Still, the locals loved the ice cream truck. And I'd found I loved working on it, even though this was a cover and not a real job.

I inhaled slowly, held it, then exhaled and held my breath again, bringing myself back to neutral.

There had been no word about my status as an agent for the NSIB. Not since I had been compromised while on assignment in Dubai. Turned out the new Crown Prince had illicit connections and he wasn't that happy that I'd figured it out.

"Barkington, hou op!" Hentie cried, in Afrikaans, her arms out to snag her dog. "This is meant to be our relaxing break time." She lifted Barkington onto her lap at the table then gave me an apologetic smile. "Sorry, April," she said. "I don't know what's his problem today."

"No need to apologize," I said, and waved a hand.

It was around ten in the morning, and now was the perfect time for a break—the day had gotten steadily hotter, and it was only a matter of time before the rush of tourists and locals started up. Another reason I was grateful Hentie had offered to help me on the truck.

*Even if you're lying to her about who you are.*

That thought was entirely true, but it didn't change

anything. The last person I'd gotten emotionally involved with had died.

I continued my breathing exercise, scanning the ocean. It was idyllic, and I wasn't going to ruin this by—

"Hey!" Hentie said, her South African accent pronounced. "Hey, you can't just come here and take over. What are you doing?"

A young woman with crimson ringlets, holding a camera, tripod, and a phone had crowded onto the bench, nudging Hentie halfway off it. She arched a tinted eyebrow at Hentie. "Relax, hon."

Barkington barked at the woman, stamping his little paws on Hentie's thighs.

I got down from the truck and went over to join them. "There a problem?"

"She half-pushed me off the bench. This is a public space, right? So you can't just—"

"Lady, you need to relax. I'm just camping out here for a couple of minutes. Trust me, I don't want to be around you and your yapping dog any more than you want to be around me and all my brilliance. So keep your darn hair on."

Hentie's jaw dropped. Barkington whined and lay down, covering his caramel-colored snout with two matching paws, and peering up at the woman.

"Excuse me," I said. "What's your name?"

"Are you serious?" The woman asked, pouting red lips that were almost the exact same shade as her hair. "You're kidding, right?"

"I'm April Waters." I gave her my cover name, of course. Even when I wasn't under cover, I tended to keep my name to myself. Delta Mission stood out.

"I'm Cressida," she said.

"What like that car?" Hentie asked.

Cressida gave her a withering look, then switched her focus to me. "Wait, you two, really don't know who I am?"

"We do now," I said. "Look, I'm sure you didn't mean any offense, but you did nearly push my friend off her seat. I understand you're probably in a rush, but you owe her an apology." And I followed that up with the Mission stare. It was a look I'd inherited from my Great Aunt, Georgina Mission, and it tended to curl toes whenever I used it. Which was sparingly.

Cressida swallowed and wet her lips then turned to Hentie. "Sorry," she said. "I didn't mean to, uh, push you or whatever. I'm super stressed right now."

"Oh, that's okay," Hentie said, tapping her on the shoulder, a bright smile parting her lips. She fluffed her messy gray bun atop her head. "Why are you stressed? Are you recording a project for your art classes or what?"

"You're both serious," Cressida laughed, and toyed with her necklace. It was ornate, with a dark chain and sparkling red stone the size of a quarter. "You actually don't know who I am?"

"Should we?" I asked. "We're from out of town."

"Oh, that totally explains it," Cressida said, twirling a hand as she talked. "I'm Cressida from the ViewTube channel, Ghostly Dares with Cressida the Queen. I run a ghost hunting channel. I'm kind of a big deal on the internet, and in this town. I'm responsible for the creation of the Graveyard Ghost Tour."

"Wait, there's a Graveyard Ghost Tour?" Hentie's eyes lit up. "April, we've got to do that."

I groaned inwardly. I wasn't a big believer in ghosts. "A ghost tour," I said, my tone flat.

"Oh," Cressida said, her eyes lighting up. She clasped her hands together in front of her chest and smiled. "You're a cynic. I love cynics. I love the looks on their faces when they get haunted for the first time."

"I'm not a cynical person," I said. "But I guess you could say I'm more of a 'see it and believe it' type of woman."

"And I," Hentie said, "had a haunted bedroom when I was a child."

"You did?" I asked.

"Oh, yeah. Shadows flitting across the walls. Growling. Things being dropped," Hentie said.

Cressida gasped. "That sounds like a Stage 5 haunting!

Or a demonic house possession. You poor thing. You must have been terrified."

"More like fascinated," Hentie said, stroking Barkington's ears. "I've always wondered how much of what I saw was my imagination."

"I can guarantee you," Cressida said, "none of it was your imagination. These things are real, and they're dangerous. You've got to have protection." She fumbled a cross on the end of a chain out from underneath her t-shirt and held it out. "See? Carry it on me at all times. That and silver bullets, just in case."

"You're going to shoot the ghosts?" I asked.

"Only in the recording sense." Cressida patted the camera beside her. "The bullets are for werewolves."

"Okay. And that's my cue," I said, pointing toward the truck, where a few customers had joined the line out front. "Hentie?"

"Coming!" Hentie got up, Barkington tucked under her arm, and smiled at the ghost huntress. "We'll come by tonight. I just have to take part in this tour."

"You're going to love it," Cressida said. "And you might even see us there. My team is serious about capturing ghost evidence, and tonight is a crescent moon. Perfect spooky atmosphere for recording."

"Huh," I said. "You'd better keep those silver bullets

on hand then." It was a joke, of course, but Cressida effected a serious expression and nodded.

"True," she said. "So true."

Hentie and I hurried toward the truck, Barkington letting out muted barks as we went. Hentie stowed him in his little crate in the corner—complete with water food, cushions, and dog toys—and we took our places behind the glistening plastic domes that covered the flavors of ice cream.

"What do you say, April?" Hentie asked. "The Graveyard Ghost Tour?"

"Sure," I said. "Why not?" It would help distract me from my worries about my cover and the lack of contact from the NSIB.

"That's the spirit!" Hentie said, then wiggled her eyebrows. "Excuse the pun."

## Two

Exploring Carmel Springs and its surroundings was a benefit of being under cover on an ice cream truck. That and I had a lot of say over the hours I worked and how I spent my time. I wasn't technically expected to make a profit, but I had to maintain the appearance of being a business owner, which meant I spent most of my time on the truck.

But this afternoon, I needed a break, and both Hentie and Barkington—possibly because he sensed her enthusiasm about the ghost tour—were full of energy.

I parked the truck in front of one of the many local bakeries in the town, and Hentie clapped her hands. "I love this country," she said. "The blue skies, the cute brick pavements—"

"Pavements?"

Hentie clicked her fingers. "Sidewalks."

"And the lampposts! Look at them, so cute with their little iron hats." She pointed at the decorative wrought-iron lamp post closest to the truck.

"You think those are nice, wait until you taste the cupcakes from this place." I lifted a finger over my steering wheel and pointed toward the bakery, with its cute striped awning and glass front door. Inside, people stood in a line at the counter or sat at round tables, waiting for their snacks and coffees.

"Fantastic," Hentie said. "We're going to need sustenance for the ghost tour tonight."

I groaned out loud this time.

"Oh come on," Hentie said. "It will be fun!" She got out of the car and went to grab Barkington from where she'd strapped him into his crate.

I got out of the truck and waited for them. Barkington barked his usual Chihuahua greeting, and we entered the bakery—Cookie's Cupcakery—and joined the line.

"We'll get a box of cupcakes," I said.

"Oh, those lemon curd tartlets sound delicious." Hentie pointed toward the chalkboard behind the glistening glass display counter.

The place was fancy but cozy, with creaking wooden

floors, mismatched upholstered chairs and white and pink striped walls. Pictures of the bay and docked lobster boats took up space on the walls, as well as an image of the happy staff, standing side by side on opening day.

The line shifted, and Barkington let out a tiny yip in Hentie's arms.

"Almost there," I said, and patted his head. Barkington licked my fingers.

"Excuse me?" One of the wait staff, wearing a pink and white striped apron that bore a half-eaten cartoon cookie on the front pocket, smiled at us.

"Yeah," I said. "Hi, we were hoping to order some cupcakes?"

The woman, young, with her hair in a blonde French braid pulled a face. "Sorry, but I have to ask you to leave."

Hentie blinked. I frowned. Even Barkington was at a loss for barks.

"Leave?" I asked. "Why? We just wanted to grab a dozen cupcakes and—"

"No pets allowed," the woman said, with an apologetic shrug. "Those are Cookie's rules."

"The baked goods are making rules?" Hentie asked.

"No, the owner," I said. "Her name is Cookie."

"What kind of a name is Cookie?" Hentie grumbled.

I patted her shoulder. "Glass houses. Stones."

She broke into an enigmatic grin. "Fair enough. But

the rule *isn't* fair at all," she directed that to the waitress. "What's your name?"

"Anne," she said. "I'm so sorry, but I have to insist. Cookie is really strict about this type of thing. No pets."

Hentie pulled herself up straight and stiff as a board, but I put out a hand. "That's fine," I said. "We'll take our business elsewhere."

"I'm so sorry," Anne whispered, then glanced toward the counter near the front. "Look, if it was up to me, this stupid rule wouldn't even exist. I love dogs. And cats. Even birds. The other day, a woman came in with her pet parrot and I had to tell her to leave too, and it caused such a scene. There were feathers everywhere."

Hentie sighed and started for the door, and I followed her, but Anne hurried along beside me. "Which car is yours?" she whispered. "If you give me your order, I'll get it for you and bring it out. Cookie doesn't need to know."

"That would be great," I said, and nodded toward the ice cream truck. "We wanted some cupcakes. Vanilla cupcakes with caramel on top."

"Oh my gosh, you're the ice cream truck girl," Anne said. "That's so awesome. I love your Mint Freeze flavor."

I sifted through my memories until I found an image of Anne's face, smiling at me as she grasped an ice cream cone. "Ah," I said. "Mint Freeze with extra chocolate on top?"

"Yeah! You remembered."

*Curse of having an eidetic memory.* And a blessing, depending on the circumstance.

"I'll bring your cupcakes out to you. Don't worry about Cookie."

"Thanks, Anne."

Hentie got into the food truck, shaking her head. I opened my door to join her, but my cellphone trilled in my pocket. There was only one person who had my number.

Special Agent In Charge Grant. Or "Uncle" as I called him whenever we had a catch-up.

"I'll be right back," I said. "Anne's going to bring the cupcakes out to the truck."

Hentie looked as if she wanted to ask questions, but I didn't let her. I scooped my phone out of the pocket of my jeans and walked off a short way then answered the phone. "Uncle," I said. "It's been so long since I've heard from you."

"I've been awfully busy, April," Grant said, and I pictured his graying mustache, the look of perpetual frustration on his face. "We've got leaks in our roof." Code for their being moles in the NSIB. "I've had trouble taking care of them."

"But your roof isn't leaking any more?"

"Nope. All clear now."

"That's great news, Uncle," I said. "I can't wait to get

home to visit." Which meant, I couldn't wait to get back to work for my government, taking on important duties that didn't include serving ice cream and going on ghost tours.

I glanced back at the truck. Though, if I thought about it, I was having a good time. Maybe too good of a time, given that I was meant to be undercover.

"I'm afraid you're not going to be able to visit any time soon. Your old friend is very unhappy with you. He's been spreading rumors around town," Grant said. "He's trying to find you with everything he has."

"And what about stopping those rumors?" I asked, this was, of course, in reference to the Crown Prince trying to hunt me down in revenge for exposing his illicit dealings and involvement in weapons deals with enemies of our country. He wanted me dead. And he had the money to see it done.

"We're working on it," Grant said. "But it hasn't been easy, and I'm afraid I don't have a solid update for you."

"Oh." That was disappointing.

"Hang in there, April," he said. "Keep out of trouble."

I bit down on the inside of my cheek. "And my family?" Talking about Gamma and Charlie wasn't strictly allowed, but I couldn't help asking. I missed them. They were the only real family I had left.

Grant sighed. "They're up to their usual shenanigans."

I smiled to myself. Of course they were. Living their best lives.

"Don't trust anyone, April," Grant said. "I don't have to tell you that people are seldom who they say they are." And then he hung up without saying goodbye. I returned to the truck to wait for the cupcakes, my stomach sinking.

# Three

We finished a delicious dinner at the Oceanside Guesthouse—Shawn and Sam had prepared a lasagna that had fulfilled my cheesy cravings—while Trouble, the adolescent ginger cat who lived at the guesthouse, teased Barkington relentlessly.

The two had become friends since Hentie had moved in a couple of weeks back.

Trouble had inspired Barkington, it seemed, as he'd taken to scratching at my door in the mornings and sneaking into my room any chance he got. The pair would hide under my bed then spring out and "attack" as one.

At quarter to eight, when the night was alive with crickets, I met Hentie and Barkington out on the front porch.

"I'm so excited," Hentie said. "This is going to be the best night ever." Barkington barked his agreement.

Both of them had oodles of enthusiasm. "Yeah. I'm sure it will be great."

Hentie tapped me on the forearm. "You just gotta get into the groove," she said. "The spooky mood. Imagine we actually see real ghosts. It's going to be lekker."

"Lekker?"

"Fun. Nice," she said.

"I don't know if lekker is what I'd call it, if that's the case," I said.

"Lighten up. It's going to be a blast."

We drove the ice cream truck out to the local cemetery and met with the rest of the ghost tour participants and our Graveyard Ghost Tour host in front of the closed cemetery gates. Wrought iron, black, and topped with palisade spikes, they were plenty creepy.

"What do they need gates like that for?" Hentie murmured, shivering and holding Barkington close to her chest. "Who are they trying to keep out of the cemetery?"

"Keep out?" I asked, and then twiddled my fingers in her direction. "I think you mean who are they trying to keep in?"

"Stop," Hentie said.

"You were the one who said I should get in the mood for spooky stuff."

"Ja, but I meant you, not me," Hentie said.

I swallowed and practiced my breathing, staring at the gates to the cemetery. It wasn't the spooky stuff that was getting to me. I didn't care about ghosts and ghouls or silver bullets and werewolves. The image of Mickey's funeral appeared in my mind, and it was a struggle to push it away.

*You're fine. You can do this.*

The ghost participants murmured and talked, huddling close together, while our host, a man in a white shirt bearing the name "Graveyard Ghost Tour" , talked on the phone nearby.

A car pulled up in the parking lot beside the truck, and Cressida got out of it, her red curls falling over her shoulders. She wore a puffy jacket. An older gentleman with gray streaks in his hair got out of the driver's side and was followed by another young woman who held camera equipment. Her hair was dank and long, hanging past her shoulders, but she wore a bright smile. "Awesome!" she exclaimed. "This is going to be the one, Cress, I can feel it."

"All right, girls, let's just relax." The guy said.

"Dad, come on," Cressida said. "You're here to help with the equipment, not give us advice. We're the Viewtubers, remember?" She gestured to the other woman and then herself.

Hentie waved at Cressida, and the three of them came

over. Cressida's father hung behind the other two, fiddling on his phone. "You've gone up another hundred subscribers," he said.

Cressida ignored him and put up a bright smile. "So you guys decided to come along."

"We couldn't resist," Hentie said. "Who's your friend?" Hentie was blunt most of the time, and I liked that about her.

"This is Macy from Macy Ghost Hunt," Cressida said. "She's a smaller Viewtuber." She sniffed. "I thought I'd throw her a bone by including her in tonight's video."

"Nice to meet you," Macy said, with a bright smile. "I can't wait for this collab to hit the Tube. People are going to go nuts."

"Another hundred subscribers!" Cressida's father lifted the phone. "Honey, wrap this up. We've got work to do."

"We'll see you in there," Cressida said, closing her hand around that fancy necklace she wore. "Try to stay respectful. Ghosts don't like it when you're rude to them."

"Of course," Hentie said, eating up every word.

I smiled and kept my cynicism to myself. It would achieve anything to show it, except to dampen Hentie's excitement, and I wasn't that type of person. I liked that she was excited about this, even if I wasn't. Besides, a night time walk would be a good distraction.

It seemed I would be in hiding for months to come.

*Even years.* My throat tightened at the thought. I'd spent my life working toward becoming the best possible spy I could be. I'd wanted to be like my Great Aunt. I'd wanted to walk in her footsteps, and for a while, it had seemed like I was on the right path.

Until I'd made the mistake of being too enthusiastic. Too interested in the Crown Prince and his friends.

My fists clenched and unfurled.

The group of content creators moved off toward the gates. They opened them and stepped through then carried on down the neat path that wound between gravestones and past trees and shrubbery.

"Hmm. That kind of kills the magic," Hentie said. "I thought the cemetery was locked."

"All right everyone," the host of the ghost tour said, clapping his hands to get our attention. "Gather round, gather round. We're going to get started in just a minute."

Hentie shuffled forward a few steps, Barkington trembling in her arms. The other ghost tour guests gathered, glancing at each other, excited or nervous or both.

"Good, good, yes." The ghost tour guy was balding, with a broad face and a smile that stretched a little too wide. "My name is Derick, and I'll be your ghost tour host this evening. Now, as many of you have realized, our tour takes place in the cemetery tonight. Tomorrow, we'll be visiting the graveyard attached to the Carmel Springs

Catholic Church, so, if you enjoy this evening's tour, be sure to join us for that."

A murmur passed through the group.

"Carmel Springs has a rich history, especially when it comes to hauntings. Some of the buildings in the old part of town are actively haunted. Carmel Springs was built specifically around the bay and the docks. In fact, one of the oldest recorded ghost sightings took place on Springs Wharf. A woman seeking her loved one—a lobsterman who was lost out at sea—haunts the wharf even to this day, with local sailors claiming they've sighted her and always around the same time."

I held back a snort.

Hentie and Barkington were wide-eyed beside me. Crickets chirped in the grass.

"But tonight, our tour will focus on the only serial killer this town has ever known."

Gasps traveled through the group.

The host opened the gates and they squealed on their hinges, clacking open. "Follow me, gentle folk, if you *dare.*" And then he walked down the path.

# Four

THE FURTHER WE GOT INTO THE CEMETERY, THE closer the group huddled together in the dark. The only light came from the ghost tour host's flashlight, and Derick took great pleasure in turning it off often, drawing shouts and gasps.

Barkington barked frantically, and Hentie had to shush him and coo to calm him down.

"Could you please stop doing that?" I asked, as Hentie grabbed hold of my arm and squeezed it painfully hard for the umpteenth time. I'd definitely have a bruise in the morning, and we weren't allowed to use our phones on the tour. Rules were rules, apparently. *And they were made to be broken.*

Derick clicked on the flashlight again, hovering it

below his chin with a comically evil smile. "Why? Are you scared?"

"I bruise like a peach," I muttered, as Hentie released my arm again.

"Ag, sorry, liefie," Hentie said, patting my arm. "It's just a bit scary, you know. There are ghosts all around us."

The only thing "around us" were the gravestones, many of them crumbling. We were far from the gates to the cemetery, closer to the edge of the treeline. Lights flashed between those trees—probably Cressida and her Viewtuber friend, making their video. Here, weeds tangled around the stones, and many of the names and dates were illegible. We'd had to enter a small iron gate to get here, and it had squealed when our host had opened it. Which had, of course, scared everyone and given me yet another bruise.

Barkington trembled and pressed his doggy body against Hentie's chest.

"You might wonder why these particular gravestones are so dilapidated," Derick said. "It's because we're in the old cemetery, which was established in the 1700s."

My eyebrows arched upward. That was pretty cool. I might not be a fan of the supernatural, but history fascinated me. The best future was brought into being by heeding the lessons of the past. Funny how I still struggled with that—but then, there was something to be said for human nature. Or just *my* stubborn nature.

"—rest of the cemetery was built onto it as the town expanded. Originally, the local church was attached to this graveyard. You can still see the ruins between the trees if you look for them."

That had to be where Cressida had gone off exploring.

*Why are you so worried about her?*

I scratched my forehead and consulted my memories. Images flickered through my mind. A clear image of Cressida talking to Hentie on the boardwalk, that red crystal glimmering against her throat. And then a fuzzier image, gloomy, with shapes I couldn't quite make out. That was odd.

What was I missing? And why did I care?

"But here we stand, near the graves of the founding members of this town. In fact, this very cemetery is rumored to be the site of the most vicious haunting in all of Carmel Springs." Derick paused for effect, glaring around the circle of tour participants.

Hentie's hand reached for my arm again, and I gritted my teeth to brace for the pain.

"You see, we're standing right beside the gravestone of Mrs. Mary McClary, the wife of one of the founders of this town. And Mrs. McClary was Carmel Springs' first and only serial killer."

Gasps.

A shot of pain in my arm from my friend's claw grip. Barkington whined and burrowed his snout into Hentie's armpit.

"Mrs. McClary killed five of the town's most influential people. The butcher, the baker, the—"

"Don't say candlestick maker," I said.

"—the cobbler, the haberdasher, and her very own husband. It's claimed that she went mad after bearing her fifteenth child."

"Of course, you'd blame it on childbirth." I rolled my eyes.

"At least she sort of replaced all the people she killed," Hentie said.

And it was so out of pocket, I burst out laughing. Everyone turned and stared at me, and Derick sniffed and cleared his throat.

"Sorry," I muttered, raising a hand.

"Mary McClary was a bloodthirsty woman. After murdering the leaders of the town, it's rumored that she stole their money and tried to bribe the local judge. And when that didn't work, she threatened to kill him. Instead, Mary wound up taking her own life under that very tree." Derick pointed toward the woods and the closest tree—an oak that stood taller than the rest. "She haunts this cemetery to this day, searching for new victims and for revenge on those who dared betray her. In fact, some of the families who still live in Carmel Springs are descendants of her enemies."

A breath of wind rustled the grass and tugged at the back of my blouse, and whispers started up from the ghost tour participants.

"Tonight," Derick said, "we're going to try to summon her to talk to us. But beware, she's rumored to be handsy when she's angry."

"That seems like a terrible idea," Hentie said.

Barkington barked and shuffled in her arms.

"It's okay, Blaffies." Hentie petted him. "It's okay, it's just a silly story. There's no reason for you to be afraid."

The words had barely left Hentie's lips when a blood curdling scream rent the air. It had come from the woods, from the direction of Mary McClary's death tree. Chaos broke out among the tour participants. People screamed. The couple next to us ran into each other in their haste to get out of the cemetery and smashed their heads together. Hentie let out a wail.

And Barkington made his bid for freedom.

"Barkington, no!" Hentie cried.

But the Chihuahua streaked off toward the trees. It wasn't the first time Barkington had made a run for it when he was stressed out, and the last time, he'd run right into a kiddies pool and I'd had to fish him out.

"I've got it," I said to Hentie. "Wait here."

I ran past the stunned ghost tour host—clearly the scream wasn't part of the tour or his plan to freak out the group—following Barkington's path between the trees.

It was much quieter between the gnarled trunks, underneath the foliage that allowed hardly any light. The moon was a sliver in the night sky, and I took my cell phone out of my pocket and turned on its flashlight, the beam arcing between the trees.

A rustling noise to my left drew my focus, and I moved in that direction. "Barkington?" I called softly. "Barkington, here boy. It's okay. Auntie April is here." It sounded strange to my ears.Maybe because I didn't like lying to Barkington. *Ridiculous.*

Footsteps shuffled to my right, and I swung the phone around, the beam slicing through the blackness and lighting up the trunks of the trees, the bark pale by the light. The hair on the back of my neck stood on end.

I didn't call out again, but I listened. The footsteps had slowed to a stop.

I covered the flashlight and stepped sideways, hiding behind a tree and listening. Footsteps again, moving toward the cemetery, away from the trees. I swung out and pinned the person in the glare of the flashlight.

Cressida's father's eyes widened and he lifted his hands

as if I were a cop. "Sorry, I'm not trespassing. I was just on my way out of the—"

"Who screamed?" I asked.

"I don't know, I—"

Frantic barks came from deeper in the trees. I took a mental snapshot of the man, bewildered, streaked in sweat, and then ran toward the noise.

*Five*

"Barkington," I said, bursting through the trees and into a clearing. "Barkington, what's—?"

But it was apparent what was wrong.

A dead body. In the middle of the forest. In between the jagged stone remains of what had once been the church walls.

Barkington sniffed around near the corpse's feet, and I swept him into my arms right away. "You," I said, "are going to get a big doggy treat when we get back to the Oceanside." I held him tight, though he didn't make a bid to escape, and trained my light on the body in the center of the ruins.

Crimson ringlets crested her head, falling across her face. She had been stabbed in the left side of her chest and lay supine on the grass.

"Quickly," I murmured, and moved toward the body. I took a mental image for later examination, and bent beside Cressida.

I pressed my fingers to her neck, but there was no pulse, not even a faint one, and her skin had already started cooling. I took a step back and scanned the scene. Defensive cuts on her hands and forearms. She had fought her attacker, or had tried to at least, and—

*The necklace is gone. The red stone.*

Could this be a robbery gone wrong? But the attack was targeted. Rage-filled.

Barkington let out a muted bark, and I backed away from the scene. Cressida's camera wasn't near her body— did that mean she had fled in this direction? That she had screamed when her attacker had found her.

If she'd been attacked from behind, she would have wounds on her back, not her front. It seemed that the attacker had approached from the same direction I had come from.

*The father?*

I backed up further, scanning the grass. I'd have to call 911 soon. The longer I stayed here, the more I contaminated the scene and would land myself in trouble for it. There were light depressions in the grass, but they weren't easy to identify, and I wasn't under any illusions about my prowess as a forensic scientist.

Movement between the trees caught my attention, and I covered my flashlight again, creeping toward the noise, Barkington tense in my arms.

There was someone still out here.

If I called the police, they would secure the cemetery, but if I caught the murderer now, before they could get away, well, that would be first prize. It would be tough when I had Barkington tucked under one arm, but I could pull it off.

I stroked a finger over Barkington's snout to calm him as I moved through the trees.

The attacker would have blood spatter on their clothes. They would have to change.

*What was the father wearing when he arrived?*

Rustling steps prevented me from paging through the images in my mind.

I rounded a tree, the flashlight still covered, and kept moving through the dark, stepping quietly, listening. The steps moved perpendicular to the scene, away from it and toward the cemetery proper—they weren't in a rush, and they weren't trying to sneak either.

Barkington, to his credit, remained silent, as if he sensed the seriousness of the situation.

I stopped, listening, then stepped out in front of the person trying to sneak away from the scene. I popped my finger away from the flashlight and blasted them in the eyes with the beam from my phone.

Macy shrieked and covered her face, jumping back a step, and dropping her camera in the process.

Instantly, I took a mental snapshot of her appearance. Her hands were clean of blood, and her shirt, though black, wasn't spattered with anything. But had she been wearing the same outfit when she'd gone into the cemetery with her crew?

That image from earlier remained frustratingly blurred.

"Macy," I said, and shifted the flashlight beam off to one side. "What are you doing here?"

She dropped her hands from her face to reveal tears, streaming down her cheeks, painted black by her mascara. Her hair was tied back in a ponytail that hung limp—she'd had her hair down before. That much I *did* remember.

"Macy?"

"I—I heard someone scream," she whispered, shakily. "I was coming to find Cressida and Royson."

"Royson's her father?"

"Yeah."

"He's already heading back to the front of the cemetery." *Shouldn't have let him go.* But at the time, I'd had no idea what I'd find in the woods. I'd only had Barkington's health and wellbeing in mind. "Why did you split up?"

"We were going to cover more ground," Macy said. "Is everything all right? I mean, I heard a scream."

"Maybe your friends got spooked." Barkington whined and cuddled closer to me. "What do you mean you three were going to cover more ground?"

Macy took a breath. "Sorry. I'm kind of weirded out because, well, I'm pretty sure I caught an EVP of a ghost near the edge of the cemetery."

"An EVP?"

"Electronic Voice Phenomenon," Macy said. "It's where you catch the disembodied voice of a person on a recording device like a phone or a camera or spirit box." She waved a hand. "And we split up as part of the video." She bent and picked up her camera, dusting it off. "Great. It's broken. The lens is cracked. Thanks for scaring me by the way." She huffed out a breath. "Why did you even *do* that? Like, I was just trying to report back to—"

"So you were at the cemetery boundary wall, right? Where was Royson?"

"He kind of doesn't record that much since he's basically Cressida's manager, and who even cares? You just made me break my camera. I'm leaving." And she pushed past me.

Or she tried to.

I caught her upper arm with my free hand, shifting Barkington so he didn't fall.

"Hey, what are you—?"

"Cressida's dead," I said.

Macy's eyes widened, then darted off to the side. "What are you talking about? That's impossible. I saw her like a half an hour ago. She's fine." She pulled away from me. "I don't know what kind of sick joke you think this is, but it's not funny. You're weird."

This was peak irony coming from the ghost hunter, but I didn't press the issue. I'd only mentioned it because I'd wanted to study her reaction. If she was the murderer, she'd already be privy to the knowledge that Cressida was dead.

Macy shuffled off, glancing back at me with an expression of disgust. "Seriously, I don't know what game you're playing, but I'm going to report you to the cops for this."

That was an empty threat.

"It sounds to me like you're trying to threaten my friend."

"Where is your friend?" I asked.

"Why would I tell you that?" She stuck out her tongue at me like a moody teenager, then stormed off.

Darn. I wasn't going to get anything out of her.

I called 911 to report what I'd found, holding Barkington close to my body, my gaze roving over the trees, trying to make out any noises that could indicate someone was sneaking through the dark around us. But there was nothing. Only silence.

And then another high-pitched scream.

That had come from the murder scene nearby.

# Six

Barkington let out a volley of yapping barks as we thundered through the undergrowth, him stiff in my arms like a doggy sentinel. If someone had found the murder scene, this would go sideways fast. The other ghost tour participants weren't exactly spies or cops or qualified to handle this type of situation. They'd contaminate the scene.

And that familiar curiosity, that need to occupy my brain with answers, to figure out the truth about what had happened, had taken hold of me.

I had to know who had killed Cressida and why.

I burst through the trees at the exact same moment as several other ghost tour participants, and our balding and now incredibly sweaty host, Derick. Gasps and shocked cries rang out, as every set of eyes turned toward the crime scene.

And Hentie.

Who stood over the body.

She wasn't bloodied, of course, and she swayed on the spot, her hand on her mouth, staring down at Cressida's corpse.

"Hentie!" I shouted it, trying to snap her out of her horrified reverie. "Hentie?"

Barkington let out three loud barks—loud for a Chihuahua—and Hentie's gaze snapped toward us. She stumbled forward, and the ghost tours participants backed away. A few of them had already fled back through the bushes. And one of the women nearest Derick had gone into a dead faint—he'd caught her before she'd hit the ground.

Hentie stopped in front of us, staring over my shoulder, paler than usual.

"Hentie?"

"Ongelooflik. Dis ongelooflik," she muttered.

I held out Barkington, right up close to her face, and he barked and licked her cheeks.

That snapped her out of it. "Blaffies?" She took him in her arms and held him close. "Blaffies. Oh, Blaffies." And then she looked at me. "April, there's— She's dead."

"I've already called the cops," I said.

"But— How? Where?"

"Did you see anyone near the body?" It was unlikely, since the killer wouldn't hang around to get caught, but it was worth asking. There was always a slim chance they would return to the scene of the crime.

"I didn't see anyone," Hentie said. "Not a soul. Not a soul." And then she burst into tears.

Barkington licked her cheeks and barked his concern.

"It's okay, Hentie. It will be okay."

Shouts rang out, and two figures emerged from the trees, their flashlights cutting through the dark. Detective White had arrived on the scene. And he was already talking to Derick while his police officers moved to cordon off the body.

BARKINGTON CUDDLED INTO HENTIE'S ARMS while she talked to Detective White's partner—he was a cop from Augusta with a pronounced scowl and a dimple right between his eyebrows at the top of his nose. It looked like target practice to me, but that kind of joke wouldn't sit well with either detective.

Detective White crunched over to me and drew me back from the scene under one of the trees, guiding me with a hand cast out and two clicks of his ballpoint pen.

"Who's the new guy?" I asked.

Detective White wasn't a bad-looking guy, shaved head and all, but the stress of being a cop had clearly worn on him. He had pronounced wrinkles on his forehead and what looked like a mean rash starting on his neck.

He scratched at it, then adjusted his lanyard bearing his identification. "I'll ask the questions, Miss Waters."

"Sure," I said. "I was just curious after what happened on the cruise ship."

"What's that supposed to mean?"

"Nothing," I said. "Just seems like... Well, it's interesting that you've got another detective working with you. Are you worried about a crime trend, Detective?"

White glanced off to the side at Derick and some of the last stragglers of the ghost tour who hadn't yet had their statements taken. He narrowed his eyes, gaze flickering to my face. "Look, the last guy who worked here, he had to retire early because he was so stressed out. He moved away, left behind his fiancé and everything."

"Oh," I said, frowning.

"And the guy before that was murdered."

"Wow."

"Yeah, so after a long period of peace and quiet in this town, you could say we're a little stressed about a sudden upswing in murders."

"Technically, the last one didn't take place in town," I said helpfully. "That was on board the ship."

"Tell that to the Chief," White muttered, then shook his head. "Detective Colson is here to help out. He's a brilliant detective." But there was a hint of derision in his tone.

"That's great news," I said. "Good to have more people around to figure this type of stuff out."

"Hmm." White clicked his ballpoint a couple of times. "Last time, you were— Uh, let's just keep you out of it, all right?"

"Not following, sorry."

"You almost got hurt the last time there was an incident," he said. "So how about you keep yourself safe."

"Look at you, worrying about a citizen's safety," I said, flashing him a bright smile.

White wet his lips. "Sure. That's the reason why." He chuckled and broke eye contact with me, whipping out a notepad.

The police had set up a few spotlights around the scene, along with a sheet to bar the body from view.

Detective White angled his pad toward the light and made a note. "So, talk to me about what happened tonight. What exactly did you hear? How did you find the body?"

I gave him as close to the truth as possible, from

chasing down Barkington, to finding the body then hearing a noise. Except I told him I'd run from the noise and found Macy. "Then I called the cops, returned to the scene, and found Hentie and the others."

"You found Hentie," he said. "You say you found her but not how you found her. I've heard it from just about everyone here that she was found standing over the body."

"I think she was in shock," I said. "She didn't kill anyone. I was with her when we heard that initial scream, and if you ask any of the others, they'll tell you that too. We all heard it together, and that's when Barkington took off between the trees."

Detective White pursed his lips.

He didn't buy it.

"Detective, I found the body before Hentie did. Cressida was already dead. I think Hentie came looking for us and stumbled upon the scene."

"For us?"

"Yes. Barkington was with me."

"Ah. And you knew the victim, it seems."

"We met her while we were on the ice cream truck this morning," I said. "She stopped to rest before she headed off to do whatever prep she needed to do for tonight."

"Prep?"

I told him about Cressida being a ghost hunting View-Tuber and how she'd stopped by this morning. I wasn't sure if Hentie would reveal their initial quarrel, but I left it out, regardless. I didn't want to land my friend in any more trouble than she was already. Not that she should've been in trouble.

She hadn't done anything wrong except come to find her pet. If anything, the cops should be more interested in me.

Detective White took my statement, told me he'd be in touch, and then moved off to the next witness on the scene. Nearby, Barkington let out a worried howl in Hentie's arms.

*Don't worry, Barkington. I won't let Hentie get in trouble.*

$S$even

THE FOLLOWING MORNING, I YAWNED AT OUR favorite table in the Oceanside Guesthouse, my eyes watering after a lack of sleep and a night spent reviewing what had happened out in the cemetery. A corkboard had formed in my mind, the image of Cressida's body in the center, thin red lines spreading outward in different directions. There were loose ends; there were pictures. That blurry image bothered me endlessly.

"Good morning, April." Sam stood beside me, holding a mug of coffee. "How did you— Oh my gosh! Are you okay?" Sam's brown eyes widened as she placed the much needed caffeine on the white table cloth right in front of my plate.

I gestured for her to sit, and she brought a polished armchair over.

The rest of the dining room was empty, but breakfast would be served shortly. The smells of baked bread and frying bacon drifted from the kitchen.

"You haven't heard about last night," I said, blocking a yawn with my hand.

Sam had been asleep at the time, but you never knew how fast news got around in small towns like Carmel Springs.

"What happened?" Sam propped her chin in her palm.

I told her, keeping it brief, occasionally breaking eye contact to glance out of the window at the dew sprinkled front lawn and the I Scream for Ice Cream truck parked and waiting—blue and pink, with a giant ice cream on top.

How obscene that we'd left a crime scene in an ice cream truck.

*Gosh, how tired am I?*

I took a sip of my coffee after I'd told Sam the story, and she sat there, agape. "Cressida's dead," she murmured. "That's— That's terrible. Who would want to kill her? She was a celebrity, for goodness' sake. She's the whole reason that ghost tour got started in the cemetery. Our Halloween festivities have improved dramatically since she started up that ViewTube channel."

I shook my head and took another sip of coffee.

"I wonder," Sam said, and sat back, tapping her pale chin. "Huh."

"What is it?"

"Cressida was... famous," Sam said, "but there were a lot of people who were jealous of her. And, apparently, she had a really strange relationship with her father."

"Strange how?"

"I heard rumors he was controlling," Sam said. "And she was in her twenties. She should have been her own woman."

"He *was* there," I said.

"See?" Sam tapped the table with her fingertips. "He's a strange man too. He's been single ever since Cressida's mother decided to leave him in the dead of the night. She left without saying goodbye to either of them."

I arched an eyebrow.

"Exactly," Sam said. "Suspicious. Where would she have gone?"

Hentie entered the dining area, wearing another of her pantsuits, though she'd chosen gray instead of a bright color. She held Barkington under one arm. "Hi," she said, in a monotone. "Sam, can I have some coffee, asseblief?"

"It means 'please'," I said, then smiled at Hentie. "See? I'm learning."

She gave me a faint glimmer of a smile before sitting down.

"I'll get that coffee," Sam said, and excused herself.

"How are you holding up?" I asked Hentie.

While I'd seen plenty of dead bodies in my checkered past, Hentie hadn't. She was a housewife who enjoyed cruises, animals that made an inordinate amount of noise, and lazy Sundays.

Hentie reached up and fluffed her messy gray bun. "I didn't get much sleep last night," she murmured. "Every time I closed my eyes..."

I squeezed her arm. "I know," I said. "I know."

Hentie sighed. "I just want to have breakfast and forget about the whole thing."

But I doubted that would happen. Hentie had been questioned by the local detective, and the folks from the ghost tour had seen her standing over Cressida's body. I tore open a packet of sugar, emptied it into my coffee and stirred a spoon through it—I needed an extra kick this morning.

Hentie drank her coffee in silence while Barkington sat in her lap, watching me with curious eyes over the rim of the table. Trouble, the inn's calico cat, was nowhere to be seen this morning.

We ate breakfast in much the same way. I wanted to console her and tell her that everything would be all right, but it would likely make things worse. Best to let Hentie forget about last night and pretend it had never happened.

After a delicious breakfast of eggs and bacon with fresh-baked bread, smeared with butter that melted instantly, Hentie and I got up from the table.

"We'll take today off," I said, as we walked through to the entryway of the guesthouse, the floorboards creaking underfoot.

"Thanks, April," Hentie said. "I need the rest." Barkington gave a much softer bark than usual. He'd had his breakfast with us, eating out of a colored bowl next to our table.

I stepped toward the front doors of the guesthouse and Hentie cleared her throat. "Going to have another secret phone call?" she asked.

I turned toward her, breathing easy and keeping my expression impassive. It would suck if I had to leave because Hentie figured out anything regarding my real identity. Killing her wasn't on the table—I would never forgive myself. Maybe that made me a weak spy, but if that was the case, so be it.

"Don't worry," Hentie said. "I'm not going to say anything to anybody. I'm not that kind of a person." And then she waved goodbye and headed down the hallway toward her room. Barkington poked his head over the side of her arm and watched me.

This was the trouble with essentially being around

someone twenty-four hours a day. She'd picked up on my habits. And I hadn't exactly told Special Agent in Charge Grant about my new truck partner. He would be livid. And his blood pressure couldn't take a knock.

I slipped out of the guesthouse and stopped on the porch. The day had already warmed, the sky was cloudless, and it was set to be another perfect summer's day in Carmel Springs. *The ghost and lobster capital of Maine.*

I planned out my next steps as I walked past the truck and took the long road that wound past the bay and the docks toward the boardwalk. My feet hit the rough boards, and I inhaled the scent of the salty sea air, casting my gaze over the blue water. I stopped near the railing and leaned on it, taking this moment for myself.

This would be the only moment of respite I'd allow myself until this murder was solved, and I'd have to be careful doing it. If I compromised my cover, I'd have to leave Hentie and Barkington behind and move on to another cover. Assuming Special Agent in Charge Grant didn't force me to go dark.

What Sam had told me had resonated.

I shut my eyes and enjoyed the gentle brush of air on my skin, the smells, the sounds.

The corkboard expanded in my mind. The picture of the body, connected to that blurry snapshot, then one of

Macy, hair tied back, indignant underneath the trees, and finally one of Cressida's father, Royson, shocked at running into me, rushing toward the exit.

Two main suspects.

"What on earth are you doing?" The rumbling tone cut across my thoughts.

# Eight

I OPENED MY EYES AND FOUND ROYSON STANDING beside me, a frown wrinkling his brow.

"Enjoying the sunshine," I said. "The weather's great."

But Royson didn't agree. My first impression of him had been vague—a well-dressed man with a classically handsome face and silver in his hair, but the morning afforded me a fresh view. His chin was weedy, his eyes small and narrowed as he swept his gaze over me, his lips drawn into a thin line.

The man didn't like me.

But I hadn't done anything to him.

*Other than see him close to his daughter's crime scene on the night of the murder.*

Not a sign of bloodshot eyes either. He'd had a good rest the night before. "How are you, Mr. ...?"

"Keene."

"Mr. Keene," I said. "How have you been? Last night couldn't have been easy for you." I pulled a sympathetic face and touched a hand to his arm.

Royson stiffened at my touch. "I saw you there," he said, his voice a hiss.

I glanced past him at the other residents and tourists who strolled along the boardwalk, stopping at stalls or entering restaurants and cafes. This was a great day to be on the truck, but there was no way Hentie would manage, and I couldn't stop my brain from ticking over last night's events.

"Why are you here, Mr. Keene?" I asked. "Did you feel like getting out of the house or—?"

"I came to find you," he said. "I wanted you to know that I know."

"And what is it that you know, exactly?"

"That you were the one who did it. I saw you heading into the forest, and the next thing... The next thing they find my daughter dead in the woods."

"Your daughter screamed before I entered the forest," I said.

Royson opened his mouth and shut it again, shaking his head.

"And you were in the woods yourself, Mr. Keene. If you're suggesting that I'm the killer based on how close I was to the crime scene, then you're going to have to take a long, hard look in the mirror. Huh. And you weren't the only one in there. Macy was there too, right?"

Royson swallowed. That suspicion had faded, but he was still guarded. "She was there. We split up."

"Yeah, she mentioned that you three had decided to try catching EMPs at different points in the cemetery." I purposefully said the acronym wrong. Last night, I'd researched what Macy had told me when I'd gotten back to the guesthouse.

"EVPs," Royson said. "They're Electronic Voice Phenomena." His eyes had lit up at the mention of the ghost stuff. "Fascinating. And yeah, we split up. Cressida was investigating the ruins with her camera, and I was catching footage in another part of the cemetery. Macy was as well."

Which confirmed what Macy had told me. But it didn't make her innocent. "Mr. Keene, I'm sorry for your loss. I can assure you I had nothing to do with this, but you don't need to trust me. The local police will take care of this."

Royson sniffed. "I don't know who else it could be," he muttered. "And now she's gone, and— What's going to happen to her channel?"

I nodded sympathetically, even though an alarm bell

had sounded in my mind. *That* was Mr. Keene's concern? His daughter's channel?

Royson hovered for a moment longer then walked off with a lift of the hand by way of greeting. He headed toward the end of the boardwalk, tucking his hands into the pockets of his jeans and gazing out at the ocean.

He'd gone from angry to strangely detached in the span of a few sentences. I took a mental snapshot of him standing there to add to the corkboard—a clearer image of how he looked in my mind's eye.

But I didn't have any evidence that could prove he was innocent or guilty. And the same was true for Macy. Both had been in the cemetery, but there could have been a third player I hadn't seen. My only choice was to do more research on who might have wanted Cressida gone.

And find that necklace. Asking Macy or Royson outright would only alert them to the fact that I was interested in investigating the crime.

It was imperative that I kept a low profile.

I started toward the entrance of the boardwalk, passing a red-and-white striped popcorn stand, and an arcade that was full of clacking, laughter, shrill songs from the games, and stopped at the sight of Hentie turning the corner.

She wore that gray suit, but her hair was messier than this morning, and Barkington was nowhere to be seen.

"Hentie?"

She spotted me and let out a cry, drawing attention from a couple waiting in line near the popcorn stand.

Hentie strode toward me, her eyes wide. "We gotta get out of here now."

"What? What's wrong? What happened?" I asked. "Where's Barkington?"

"I left him in my room where it's safe," Hentie said. "We have to leave."

"Leave?"

"This town. Now. Before it's too late." Hentie glanced over her shoulder and clasped her hands together. "Now, now. As in right now."

"Whoa, slow down. Tell me what happened."

"I—" She gulped. "I was about to settle down to sleep when I heard a noise outside. I'm feeling jumpy after all that stuff that happened last night, so I decided let me just check, you know, to be sure that there's nothing funny going on." Hentie shifted her weight from one foot to the other. "And I checked, and it was the cops."

"Huh?"

"The cops are at the guesthouse," Hentie said. "Both of them. Detective White and the other one. The new guy."

"Detective Colson?"

"Ja."

"All right," I said. "But you—"

"I climbed out of the window."

"You're not serious," I said.

She grabbed both my arms. "Look at me, April," she said, her eyes wide, the left one twitching. "Do I look not serious to you?"

"You look a little bit crazy, if I'm honest."

"I'd rather be crazy than in cuffs. Listen, I don't know what prisons are like here, but where I come from, you don't want to go to prison. It's a life-ender, in more ways than you can imagine. I can't go to prison. I can't—"

"Hentie, you didn't kill anyone," I said. "You're not going to prison."

"If I get in trouble, they might deport me."

"But you're married to a guy from Texas."

"Right. Right, I forgot about that." She pressed her hand to her forehead. "I suppose you're right."

A police siren whooped at the entrance to the board-walk, and Hentie froze—except for her left eye, which started twitching uncontrollably again. Some people didn't do well with the police.

"Hentie, take a deep breath. Nothing bad is going to happen to you, okay?" I whispered. "If they ask to talk to you, just go with them. And if you feel uncomfortable or they read you your rights, you request a lawyer. Don't answer a single question. Refuse them answers if you're under arrest. Got it?"

She'd gone pale, but she nodded that she understood.

"I'll go back to the guesthouse and look after Barkington."

Detective White strode over to us. "Good morning, ladies. Mrs. Cooper, would you mind coming down to the station with me? I have a few questions to ask you."

Hentie turned slowly, eye still twitching, and faced the detective, who immediately recoiled. "Oh my. Uh, do you need medical attention, Mrs. Cooper?"

"I'm f-f-f-fine," Hentie said thinly. "Am I under arrest?"

"No, ma'am. We just wanted to clarify a few things." He gestured back to the squad car where the swarthy and tall Detective Colson waited.

Hentie gulped and followed the detective to the car, glancing back at me every other step.

# Nine

Barkington sat in my lap in my bedroom, shaking like he'd survived a storm. Really, he was warm, but dogs were intuitive, and he was probably worried about Hentie. He'd likely picked up on her strange behavior. Climbing out of a window was new for Hentie, even if she was eccentric.

"It's all right, Barkington," I said, stroking his head.

I had crossed my legs and taken up a spot on the comfy white sheets in my bedroom, my curtains thrown wide to let in as much sunlight as possible.

The best thing I could do for Hentie was research the case and keep Barkington happy while the detective's questioned her.

"There, there." I kept petting him as I scrolled on my laptop.

The first port of call had been Cressida's ViewTube channel. She had a substantial amount of followers, over a million.

There were no posts about her passing, likely because the cops had told Mr. Keene not to comment on what had happened.

I clicked and organized the videos by most popular, then scrolled down the list.

Surprisingly, Cressida didn't have that many videos— ten total—but they were all labeled with exciting titles.

***Finding a Real Ghost in Carmel Springs, Maine!***

***EVP Caught on Camera. You Won't Believe What We Found?!!??***

***Ghost in Old Haunted Mansion: Real and True!***

I snorted under my breath and clicked on the last entry. "You know, Barkington, in all the years I've been who I am," I said, "I've never watched a video like this."

The video played, opening with a shot of a mansion, covered in half-dead ivy creepers and with shattered windows. Cressida's voice was a whisper. "Hey, what is up guys, it's your girl, Cressida from Ghostly Dares with Cressida the Queen, and I have a crazy video for you today." She turned the camera and pointed it at my face. "We're at the most haunted house in Carmel Springs. Like, this place is basically condemned, and we're going to try to catch some amazing footage of ghosts today. And by try, I mean we're definitely going to. Like, without a doubt."

Barkington had stopped trembling. He whined and tilted his head to one side, watching the screen with me.

"You see, this is not the first time we've been here. The last time, we caught actual footage of a woman's voice. Can you believe that? It's so crazy. A disembodied woman's voice. But I'm getting ahead of myself here," Cressida said, with a bright smile. She touched her fingers to that red crystal necklace, swallowed, and continued. "You see, the reason this is such a hotspot for ghost activity is because it's the original house of Mary McClary, the first Carmel Springs serial killer. And the last, let's hope. Haha."

That sentence was disconcerting given Cressida's fate.

"Anyways," she said, crunching through grass as she approached the house, the camera shaking slightly. "Apart from the disembodied voice, the last time we were here, we found this." Cressida lifted the necklace. "And ever since we picked this up on this site... Oh gosh, I've been going through it y'all. Like, I'm cursed. This necklace is literally cursed. I wake up every night to the sounds of scratching on my walls."

I frowned.

"And I see dark figures everywhere," Cressida whispered. "So, I'm here alone this time to give the necklace back to the house. I can't take it any more."

"Hmm," I said, pausing the video as Cressida swung the camera around and focused it back on the front of the house. "Surely a ghost hunter would have recorded these shadows and noises, right?" I duplicated the tab on my browser and navigated back to her ViewTube homepage.

Nope. No videos showing the horrifying apparitions in her home.

I pressed play and watched as Cressida approached the house. "It's almost sunset, guys. Look how creepy this— Oh my gosh! What was that?" The camera was pointed up at the top floor windows, where curtains hung limp.

Clearly someone else had lived in this house after Mary McClary. Unless Cressida expected me to believe those were Mary's original drapes?

The video slowed and rewound, and a voiceover from Cressida started up. "I had to slow down the video here so that you could see what I saw. If you look carefully at the top window, you can see that while the window is closed, the curtain moves on its own, almost as if someone is peeking out then darts out of sight. Watch again."

The video slowed even further, and a red circle appeared over the curtain in question. And it did look like someone had shifted the curtain.

Barkington let out a bark.

"Don't worry," I said. "She's probably got someone in there doing that. Or there's a squatter."

Which was pretty scary. What if Cressida hadn't disturbed a spirit in that house? What if she'd upset a resident?

My eyes narrowed and I tapped my mousepad to pause the video.

A resident who wanted their necklace back?

But to murder Cressida for it? I wasn't so sure about that.

I needed to know more about this necklace and this house. If Cressida had found that necklace in this allegedly haunted house, then it was high on my list of clues.

Another bark from the Chihuahua.

"You're not serious," I said. "You want to watch more of this?"

Barkington snuffled and scratched in my lap.

"Fine." I hit play.

Cressida let out the appropriate shocked cries at the right times, claiming she'd been touched and pulled on. The house was empty, apart from those conveniently draped curtains, most of the other windows boarded up, and the floor itself looked rotten and like a health hazard.

"That's the place, Bark," I said. "That is the place. We've got to go check it out."

I scrolled through Cressida's videos, my certainty

growing. Three of her ten videos had been shot at that same house. And for an allegedly abandoned house, it was interesting that there was no furniture. A few of the walls had spray painted words, none of which bore repeating, as well as peeling wallpaper, but there wasn't a lot of trash around or evidence of someone living in the home.

But that curtain had moved.

*Don't start. Soon enough, you'll start buying into the ghost stories too.*

There wasn't a risk of that.

A knock rattled on my bedroom door.

"Come in," I called.

Hentie shuffled into the room sans eye twitches.

Barkington let out a volley of excited barks and wagged his tail. Hentie collected him, hugging him to her chest and taking a deep inhale of his fur. "Dankie, April," she said. "I was worried about him."

"He's fine," I said. "We were doing research together. Are you okay? How did it go?"

Hentie burst into tears.

*Ten*

Barkington whined and licked Hentie's cheeks out of concern.

"Oh, Hentie," I said, and set my laptop aside. "Don't worry, it's going to be okay. Everything will be okay." I got up and gave her a hug, then grabbed a box of tissues from the coffee table in the mini-living room suite and brought it over. "Here. Dry your eyes, Henite. This isn't over."

She blew her nose loudly, and Barkington yapped.

"Sorry," Hentie said, patting underneath either eye. "I don't know why I'm so tense."

"You saw a dead body yesterday," I said. "That's shocking. There are hardened police detectives who can't handle something like that."

Hentie sniffled and stroked Barkington.

"Did they press you for information?" I asked.

"Ja. Detective Colson was mean about it too."

"They don't have anything on you," I said. "You want to take things into your own hands?" *Don't. You're not supposed to involve her.*

If I let Hentie see me in action, she would grow suspicious of me. That or I'd have to snoop like a regular person and not like one who had a special set of skills.

"What do you mean?" Hentie asked.

Barkington tilted his head to study me, held closer to Hentie's chest.

"We'll have to leave Barkington behind," I said.

"Behind for what? What do you have planned, April?"

I grabbed the laptop and turned it so that she could see the screen. "I've been doing some sleuthing in my spare time. The fact that you were so upset about the cops talking to you got me thinking."

"What, that I'm a murderer?"

"Of course not," I said. "It got me thinking that we could find the real murderer."

Hentie's bright green eyes lit up with excitement. "You want to snoop?"

"Yeah," I said. "I researched Cressida's ViewTube channel, and I found out where she got that necklace. It was at this house." I gestured to the freeze frame on the screen.

"Why does the necklace matter?"

"Because it's missing," I said. "Whoever killed her snatched that necklace off her throat."

Hentie gasped.

"So," I said, "do you want to visit a haunted house with me?"

WE TOOK THE ICE CREAM TRUCK TO THE haunted house—relatively easy to find since it was marked on the Graveyard Ghost Tours website as "Mary McClary's Haunted House." It was tucked in a back road far back from the bay at the end of an overgrown road.

I parked in front of the gates, which were wrought iron and chained shut, and Hentie and I exchanged a glance.

"Creepy," Hentie said.

"I thought you loved this kind of stuff."

"After last night? Not so much," Hentie said.

"It's late afternoon. I'm sure all the ghosts are sleeping."

"That's not how it works." Hentie lifted her chin. "Ghosts never sleep. They're cursed to roam the earth for all eternity, until they fulfill their final wish."

That was a lot to unpack. "Well," I said, "let's go see if

Marcy McClary's around. Maybe she's responsible for all of this."

Hentie's eyes widened. "Don't even say that! What if it's true?"

"Come on, Hentie."

I opened the ice cream truck door and got out into the overgrown grass specked with weeds. It wasn't like we could be inconspicuous in a truck with a giant ice cream cone on the top, so I wasn't too worried about us leaving tracks. It didn't look like anyone cared about this place anyway. And if we were confronted by the cops, we'd say we were ghost-hunting.

"The gate is locked," Hentie said.

"There's got to be a way in." We circled the barrier wall until we reached the back of the double story house. The gate at the back, smaller than the ones at the front, was damaged and falling half off the wall. I opened it for Hentie and we walked into the back yard.

It was as overgrown as the exterior, with a large crop of weeds growing out of the drain pipe near the stairs that led up to the back porch. "There," I said, gesturing to the back door. "Let's get inside."

Hentie followed me. "This is so exciting," she whispered. "You know, I always wanted to live a life of adventure when I was growing up."

"Wish granted," I murmured, and reached through the

broken window to unlock the back door. It took a turn of a rusty key in the lock inside. I bumped the wooden back door, swollen from years of ill repair, and it scraped across the floor of a scullery.

"We're in," Hentie whispered, dramatically, and squeezed past me.

"Don't touch anything."

"Right, we might leave behind fingerprints," Hentie said, twiddling her fingers at me. "Ooh! Or disturb the ghosts."

"No. You might get tetanus."

Hentie chuckled then stopped, frowning. "Why's there nothing in this place?"

The sinks were empty, and there wasn't a dishwasher or anything of note. I moved through to the kitchen. No table or chairs, nothing. It was as if the previous resident had simply moved out. Intriguing.

"Careful on the floors," I said. "They're rotting."

Hentie and I navigated through the kitchen toward the living room. There were stairs off to one side, facing the front door, but they were impassable. A good thing too, since it prevented Hentie from exploring up there and falling right through the floor.

"Hey, April," Hentie said. "What's that?"

My friend pointed toward a pile of clothing in the corner. My eyes widened. I hadn't brought my latex gloves with me because it would have seemed suspicious to Hentie if I whipped them out. I walked over, my pulse rising, and practiced my breathing.

I took a mental image of the clothing as I bent and examined them. I reached out.

"Wait!" Hentie cried. "Here. Put these on." She held out a pair of blue latex gloves.

"Where did you get those?" I asked.

"I bought them. It's always good to have a pair of gloves. I don't like germs," she said.

I laughed and took them from her. I slipped on the gloves and lifted the piece of clothing. It was a hoodie, printed with the word's Queen Cressida on the front, and a crown. "It's merch," I said. "ViewTube merch for Cressida's channel."

"Is there blood?"

"Doesn't look like it," I said, but my gaze had moved past the hoodie to the backpack on the floor. "Huh. What's this?" I lifted the pack and unzipped it. Both Hentie and I peered inside.

"Water," Hentie said.

"And snacks. A camera too. And a wallet." I opened the wallet and rifled through it. "This is two thousand dollars, at least."

"And what about the camera? Is there any recordings on it or stuff like that?"

I lifted the camera and powered it on. "Battery is nearly full. Nothing recorded."

"What is this?" Hentie asked. "I don't understand."

"This looks like someone's stash," I said. "But what for?" This didn't seem related to the necklace. Could this have belonged to Cressida? But why would she need a stash of clothing and cash? She had the money she needed from her ViewTube channel.

I layed the stuff out and took a picture with my phone, then stowed it in my pocket. I returned everything to where I'd found it, then rose, just as the scullery door creaked open.

## Eleven

Hentie covered her mouth with her hand and spun toward the kitchen doorway. To her credit, she didn't take a step or make a single noise.

The sound of sniffling penetrated the house, and I rose, silent as a cat, and stepped across the boards to join my friend. I stripped off the gloves quietly and pocketed them, just as a woman walked under the kitchen archway and into the living room.

She was pretty, with a blonde French braid hanging over one shoulder, but the image was marred by the bloodstains down the front of her white buttoned shirt.

*Anne.* From Cookie's Cupcakery.

Anne stopped dead at the sight of us standing in the living room, tears streaking her cheeks. "What are you—?"

"Is that blood?" Hentie asked. "Oh my gosh, it's

blood! She did it. It was her. She's the murderer, and this is where she's hiding her getaway stash. Quick, April. Get her!"

"Hentie," I murmured. "Take a breath."

Shouting that a suspect was covered in blood was a great way to get Anne to run like her freedom depended on it. Because it did.

"Huh?" Anne wiped the tears from her cheeks then brought a crumpled tissue from her pocket and dabbed her nose with the end of it. "What are you— Oh! Oh, no, this isn't blood," she said, and plucked at the front of her shirt.

"Liar!" Hentie cried. "I'm calling the police. They're going to take you away for a long time for what you did to poor Cressida."

"I didn't do anything to Cressida," she said. "And this is food coloring. From the bakery? Where I work?" The tears welled up and spilled over again. "I can't believe this. As if this day couldn't get any worse. Now you're here at my private spot, accusing *me* of murdering one of my favorite—" She cut off and turned away from us.

*One of her favorite what? ViewTubers?*

Hentie and I exchanged a quick glance, and I gave a tiny shake of my head.

We weren't going to catch her out if we attacked her directly. I patted the air, gesturing for Hentie to remain calm, then approached Anne. "What's going on, Anne? Why are you here?"

Anne swung around suddenly, and Hentie let out a shrill scream.

"She's attacking!" Hentie cried.

I'd already taken in Anne's posture, and it didn't speak of an attack. She was a young woman in distress, but what was she doing here?

I took another of my mental pictures. Anne standing in the middle of the ruined living room, with its peeling wallpaper, her shirt stained with splodges of red, and her makeup streaked from her tears.

"Anne?" I prompted.

I could tell she wasn't in the frame of mind to "attack" if she was capable of that, but that didn't mean I'd let my guard down.

"I could ask both of you the same question. What are you doing here?"

"You said this was your spot." I evaded her question. "What did you mean by that?"

"I meant exactly what I said. This is my place. The place I come to when I want to relax. I like it here because it's quiet and there's no one else around. Nobody knows about this place."

But that wasn't true. This was part of the ghost tour now.

Pieces of the puzzle clicked in my mind.

The necklace. The EVPs at this house.

"Are you living here?" Hentie asked, before I could find a more delicate way to phrase the question.

"What? No. I live on Berry Lane. As if I would live in this dilapidated place."

"Then what's all this stuff, huh?" Hentie gestured to the backpack and clothing. She was on a roll, and while her approach was blunt, to put it lightly, she *was* getting answers out of Anne.

Anne who hadn't even been on my radar until now. A server at one of the local bakeries? What were the chances that she was the murderer? Then again, Cressida had been so well known, it was possible.

The suspect walked over to the backpack, frowning, and studied it. "No, this is not my stuff. I have no idea how this got here." She bent and looked at it, notably, not touching it. "That's weird. I would never leave stuff here."

"But you come here all the time?" I asked. "Are you okay, Anne? You were crying."

Anne puffed out her lips and sobbed. She dabbed underneath her nose again. "I nearly lost my job today. Cookie is so awful! She screamed at me because I distracted her while she was working on the buttercream frosting for this morning's cupcakes, and then, when I tried to apologize, she threw food coloring at me and told me to get out of her bakery for the day."

"But she didn't fire you, right?"

"No," Anne said. "No, she didn't fire me. I still have my job at least, but this is crazy. She's a total tyrant. If I had it my way, I'd open my own bakery and serve the people of this town fairly. And I'd make it a pet cafe too. You know, after I brought those cupcakes out to you in your ice cream truck, one of the other servers ratted me out! I got in trouble for it. I've got two strikes." She lifted two fingers. "Third strike and I'm out."

"These things have a way of working themselves out," I said. "Don't worry."

"They do?" Anne asked. "How?"

"Karma," I replied.

"Doesn't believe in ghosts, but believes in karma, eh?" Hentie's words made me grin.

Anne finished dabbing her nose and stuck the tissue back into the pocket of her jeans. "What are you guys doing here?"

"We heard this house was haunted," I said, before Hentie could say anything and give the game away. "Mary McClary's house."

"Oh? Right, yeah, I heard about that."

But if she'd heard about it, why had she told us that this was her spot and nobody came here?

I gave her a quick smile. "This was kind of boring," I said, with a shrug. "We thought we were going to find some ghosts out here, but there's nothing. We can't even go upstairs."

"Yeah, you shouldn't," she said. "I tried once and I nearly fell through the ceiling. It was pretty scary."

"We'll see you around, Anne," I said, then gestured for Hentie to follow me out. "Feel better."

"Thanks," she sighed, and walked over to the front window. "I guess I'll leave too. I was coming out here to cry, be alone, that kind of thing, but I guess there's no point in staying now that you guys have cheered me up."

"That's great news," I said, and then Hentie and I exited through the back door.

We made quick work of heading back to the truck. Once we were inside, Hentie let out a breath. "She's the murderer," she said. "I'm sure she's the murderer. You saw how she acted! She was so suspicious she couldn't even keep a straight face. Or her story straight. She was all over the place with that stuff. First, she says, okay, ja, she's here because nobody comes here, but then she says that she knows that people come here for the ghosts." Hentie tapped on the dashboard and pointed at the house. "And where's her car? Lekker lieg. That means she's lying."

I started the truck and reversed out of the driveway. "I think you're right, Hentie. She's up to something."

"And we're gonna find out what."

*Twelve*

THAT AFTERNOON, HENTIE AND I RELAXED AFTER our encounter with Anne. Hentie's gut feeling was right. Anne was up to something, but I had to figure out what it was. She'd mentioned her house on Berry Lane, but I had to wait until nightfall before I enacted "the plan."

I'd gathered what spy tech I'd been afforded by Special Agent in Charge Grant. Which wasn't much since I was on the run, but a few high tech items were better than nothing. I'd packed the items into my utility belt, also known as a fanny pack, ready for tonight's adventure.

In the meantime, I left Barkington and Hentie to their afternoon nap, and excused myself to go "for a walk."

It just so happened that my walk took me directly past Cookie's Cupcakery.

The stroll through Carmel Springs refreshed my

senses. The summery scent of flowers mingled with the ocean breeze, and the town itself was full of stores with glass-front windows and displays. There were a lot of antique shops, bakeries, and places to eat, obviously, but I liked that. Fliers were tacked to lampposts, many of them announcing local fairs, workshops or classes, and most locals I passed by greeted me with a smile.

Though, a few of them grumbled at the sight of me, likely because they thought I was a tourist.

I reached Cookie's Cupcakery with its striped awning and cute decor, and sat down on a bench outside to rest, playing on my phone while I watched the place.

The door to the bakery clapped open, a bell tinkling above it, and a middle-aged woman exited, leading with her nose. She reminded me of a dachshund, but less cute, mostly because of the expression on her face.

"And what do you think *you're* doing?" she asked.

I looked over my shoulder. "Hi," I said, once I was sure she was directing herself at me. "Can I help you?"

"The more prudent question here is whether I can help you?"

"Uhhh?"

"Here I am spending all day making cupcakes and cookies and treats of the finest kind, and folks like you roll up and sit down on my bench and take up my sunlight," she said. "Do you really think you can—"

"Ma'am, this is a public sidewalk," I said.

"Don't you talk to me with that mouth."

"As opposed to talking to you with…?"

"I don't need back chat from the likes of you," she said, taking another step forward. "I know who you are. Don't think that I don't know who you are."

"Uh?"

"The ice cream truck girl with her annoying dog who likes to get around the rules." She circled her finger in the air.

"You must be Cookie," I said.

"I am," she said. "And I'm right out straight, so you'd better get out of here."

"Right out what?"

"Busy! I'm busy," Cookie shouted.

"Then you should probably go back inside and be busy," I replied. "Look, it's a free country." A country I'd spent years protecting and serving. "And I'm just enjoying the sunshine." And I wanted to see if Anne came back to work, or if I could talk to one of the other servers, but now that Cookie was here I didn't have to.

She drew herself upright and puffed out her chest. "You don't talk to *me* that way," she said. "How dare you!"

"I'm friends with Anne," I said. "I heard you threw food at her today."

"I didn't throw food at her. What vicious lies has she been spreading? I'll—"

"She said you were angry at her for distracting her, but you know what? You're probably right. I think Anne needs help," I said. "She's been confused lately."

That took the wind out of Cookie's sails. "Confused? What do you mean, confused?"

"I ran into her today and she was covered in food coloring, and she wasn't talking sense. Does she always act that way?"

"That girl is a thorn in my side. The way I've tried to help her and she just... Oh gosh, she does tend to babble on about crazy things when the mood takes her," Cookie said, her expression softening.

"What kinds of things?" I asked, leaning in, my eyes wide, feigning interest in the juicy gossip. Gossip with the currency in small towns and Carmel Springs was no different.

Cookie wriggled her nose. "Ghosts and spirits and made up things."

*Bingo.* Anne was a fan of Cressida. That was what she'd meant when we'd run into her this morning.

"It's ridiculous, her believing that— Oh, here we go again." Cookie gestured toward the street, and I turned around.

A crowd of teens had gathered in the street opposite,

and were talking and taking pictures with Macy, the ghost hunter. She'd combed her hair back from her face, the dark locks still looking a tad on the greasy side. She held up a peace sign and pouted her lips as she took picture after picture.

Cookie sniffed. "This darn town is going to heck." And then she turned on her heel and walked back into her bakery. The door slammed hard.

Macy continued taking pictures, but eventually the teens drifted off and left her on her own. Macy wore a self-satisfied smile as she crossed the street. Until she laid eyes on me.

She sniffed and tried to walk past me, but I cleared my throat. "Hi Macy. How are you?"

"I'd be better if I didn't have to make conversation with *you*."

"We got off on the wrong foot," I said. "But I wanted to talk to you and offer my condolences for your loss. This must be a difficult time for you."

Macy whipped around. "What's your angle? What do you actually want? The last time, it was to accuse me of a heinous crime. So what is it now? You want a photo with me that you can sell online? Is that it? You want me to sign an autograph?"

*Wow.* "Actually, I wanted to know how you are and, uh, also, what you know about Cressida's cursed necklace," I said. "There are rumors spreading around town that it might be the real cause for her death."

Macy snorted. "That's ridiculous. Cressida bought that necklace at a jewelry store in town. It was nothing special."

"It wasn't?"

"No, she told everyone it was cursed and that she found it at some old house when really, it was fake. All of that stuff's fake," Macy said. "Come on, a cursed necklace?"

"So that's fake but not the ghosts?"

Macy's face went slack. "No comment." And then she left me standing there outside the angry baker's store, contemplating.

Secrets. So many secrets, and I was fascinated by them. I took a snapshot of Macy's retreating back for the corkboard. She was still a suspect, as was Cressida's father, but Anne had made it onto the list. The fact that she'd been at the house, and that getaway stash? And she was a fan of Cressida's?

There was more to this, and I was going to peel back the layers of mystery, carefully. Quietly. And nobody would know I was involved.

## Thirteen

It wasn't difficult to find out where Anne lived—224 Berry Lane. People in town were chatty, and with the news of the murder floating around town, everybody had something to say.

I played it cool at the dinner table with Hentie and Barkington, and we enjoyed a dinner of crab cakes with blueberry pie for dessert. Barkington and Trouble played underneath the table together, occasionally darting out—Trouble to bat at people's legs and Barkington wagging his little tail and turning in a circle.

I pretended to be exhausted, it was partly true, and retired to my room.

The inn settled into the quiet night.

At around eight, I strapped on my utility belt, cleverly disguised as a fanny pack, and carefully opened the window beside my bed. I swung my leg over the sill and slipped out of the Oceanside.

I kept out of the circles of light from the lampposts and remained on foot. Tonight was about keeping everything under the radar, and I couldn't take the I Scream for Ice Cream truck.

The walk to Berry Lane was quick. The suburb it was situated in was further back from the bay, and the street itself was filled with quaint shiplap homes, doors painted different colors, with neat gardens and smooth lawns.

I strolled down the sidewalk and found Anne's house. The lights were on inside, the curtains drawn, and the houses on either side were quiet. I checked my surroundings then hopped the picket fence and moved down the side of the house.

The house was quiet, except for the sound of the TV from somewhere near the front.

It didn't seem like Anne had any friends over, which worked just fine for me. The fencing along the side of the house was slatted and taller than at the front, which afforded me privacy for what I had to do next.

I found a spot near the steps that led up to the kitchen door, and unzipped my fanny pack. I retrieved a tiny silver ball from inside, about the size of the tip of my pinky finger, and squeezed it gently.

It clicked open, the top half of the sphere swiveling

sideways on unseen hinges, revealing a tiny silver fly within. I removed the corresponding wand controller from within the fanny pack, twisted the ends, clicked, and the fly immediately lifted into the air.

A small holographic screen appeared above the wand, showing me the fly drone's view of the back yard. I tapped and twisted into night vision mode and the fence lit up in green hues.

*Perfect.*

I got comfortable in the grass then directed the fly up and around the perimeter of the house.

This drone was incredibly specific. It wasn't the type I could control from inside the truck, and had a much shorter range than any of the other fly drones I had encountered in the past. It was cheaper, though, and a concession from Special Agent in Charge Grant, since I didn't technically need a fly drone when I was in hiding.

I flew the drone back over the house, found the chimney, and sent it down into the house. At the last second, just before entering the well-lit living room, I twisted the wand and removed the night vision setting.

Inside, Anne was on the sofa, eating popcorn and watching a movie.

No. Not a movie.

She was watching Cressida's ViewTube channel, a blank look on her face as she chewed mechanically.

I tapped the wand and set the fly drone to capture images that would instantly sync to the cloud for later review. Then, I guided it through the single story home, through the kitchen, down the hall, searching for anything suspicious.

Framed pictures in the hall caught my attention, and I slowed the drone to a hover in front of them.

*Hmmm. What's this?*

The image showed Anne standing beside Cressida's father, Royson. He had his arm around her shoulders, and on Anne's other side was an elderly woman in a wheelchair.

I frowned. Anne had been that close with Cressida's family?

My instinct had been to pin her as a stalker who wanted to get rid of Cressida, but this was something else entirely. She had a direct connection to the victim.

I flew the drone further down the hall and into the main bedroom, searching for more evidence, and switching to night vision. The bed was made neatly, the closet was closed, but Anne's dressing table held an assortment of makeup and more pictures tacked to the mirror. It reminded me of my bedroom in high school, though the pictures hadn't been of friends. I hadn't had many.

Where Anne had images of smiling faces, I had had

images of guns, cars, and tech. Anything else would've angered my mother.

I flew the drone closer and hovered again.

The pictures, polaroids and printed digital images, showed Anne with friends from the bakery. But there was one image in particular that drew my focus. Cressida and Anne standing together, laughing. And Anne was wearing the necklace.

*How long ago was this picture taken?*

The bedroom light clicked on, casting a white hue over the room, and I hastily switched the drone out of night vision, and flew it past Anne's head. She was entirely unaware, yawning as she walked toward her bed.

She paused for a second, touching her hand to her neck, and glanced over at the dressing table, then went to her bed and plopped down face first into the pillows.

Clearly somebody had been having a bad day.

Not as bad as Cressida's, though.

I guided the drone back up the chimney and held out my palm. I landed it on my index finger, then switched off the wand with a few taps, and deftly scooped the fly back into its silver receptacle. A few clicks later and everything was packed away again.

I waited the appropriate amount of time for Anne to fall asleep, then crept down the side of the house and started my journey back toward the Oceanside.

Fascinating.

Anne wasn't just suspicious. She'd had that necklace before Cressida. She was close with the victim's family, and she had been crying and arrived at the Mary McClary house where we'd found the secret stash.

Questions. So many questions.

Why was there a secret stash? Who had it belonged to?

Was Anne a stalker? Or a friend? How did the allegedly fake necklace factor into this case?

Once I arrived back at the guesthouse, I slipped through the window, shut it and pondered the corkboard as I freshened up and changed into my cotton PJs before bed.

Another image had appeared, a thread connecting to the central picture of the crime scene. Anne wearing the necklace, holding Cressida and smiling brightly. Another thread connected that picture to the one of Royson on the boardwalk when he'd confronted me.

The entire family had secrets, and I had to figure out what they were if I wanted to get to the bottom of this mystery.

Troubled scratched at my bedroom door, and I let him in. The cat sauntered into my room like he owned the place, which he technically did, and then leaped up onto my bed and stared at me expectantly, as if to ask me what I was waiting for.

I got the feeling I had a long, sleepless night ahead.

## Fourteen

The following morning, I joined Hentie and Barkington for breakfast at our favorite table in the Oceanside. Hentie was more cheerful now that we'd taken matters into our own hands, and she sipped her coffee enthusiastically.

"Ja, that's what I think, hey?"

I blinked, focusing on her. I'd been mulling over Anne's connection to Cressida's family and the necklace. "What did you say, sorry?"

Barkington let out a bark and tapped his little paws in his Hentie's lap, gaze fixed on me.

"Relax, Blaffies," Hentie said, and petted his head. "She wasn't ignoring us."

"I was lost in thought. My bad."

"I was just saying that I think it's that Anne girl. She's

got to be the one who did it. Why else was she there at that house?"

"I'm not sure. The only problem is, we have to place her at the scene of the crime, otherwise it doesn't matter what we think about her," I said. "We can't prove that she did it."

Hentie picked up a piece of toast and scraped butter across it with the flat of her knife. "True, true," she said, holding the toast out of Barkington's reach. "But how do we do that?"

I lowered my voice and told her about the necklace—that there was a possibility that there'd been more than one, and that it had been a 'fake' cursed necklace according to Macy.

"And it seems like Macy is gaining a lot of popularity now that Cressida's passed on," I said. "We can't rule her out as a suspect." I took a sip of my coffee, pulled a face, and stirred one spoon of sugar into it.

"We can talk to that jewelry shop owner on our lunch break," Hentie said, and received immediate agreement from Barkington.

"That sounds like a great idea." It was a perfect summer's morning, and we had to get on the ice cream truck today. There was no point having the cover of an ice cream truck owner if I didn't sell ice cream. Besides, I was in the mood for a scoop of Mint Freeze today.

The doors to the kitchen swung open and Sam emerged, wearing her cute blue apron that didn't suit her frown. She made a beeline for our table. "Ladies," she said. "Are you okay?"

"Huh?" I looked up at her. "Why do you ask?"

Sam brought her phone out of her pocket and placed it on the table. "The local newspaper just published an article about you."

My skin went cold and prickles traveled down my spine. "About who?"

"Hentie," Sam said. "Oh gosh, I'm so sorry." She gnawed on the corner of her lip.

Hentie gulped. We were moments away from more eye-twitching, I could just tell, so I grabbed the phone, spun it toward myself and started reading.

**_Tourist Interviewed in Connection to Death of ViewTube Star._**

The title wasn't too damning, but I scanned the article. Hentie was mentioned by name. Her full name. Mrs. Hentie Cooper. Who worked on the I Scream for Ice Cream Truck.

This wasn't good.

"It doesn't say too much about the details," I said, after a quick read through. "Just your name, that you work on the truck, and that you were questioned. There are no accusations."

"Scroll a bit further down," Sam said softly.

I inhaled sharply. "It mentions that you were found standing over the body."

Hentie's eye twitch came on in full force then.

I reached across the table and patted her arm. Barkington licked the side of her hand, though I got the feeling he was angling for the crumbs on her fingertips, and Sam made cooing noises and patted her on the shoulder.

The couple who were seated closest to us in the dining area kept sending furtive glances toward the table.

"Hentie, I promise, everything will—" But the shrill ring of my phone sent anxiety racing through my veins. I got up. "I've got to take this. Excuse me." Both Hentie and Sam gave me bewildered looks, but I reassured them with a smile and moved out of the dining area.

Special Agent in Charge Grant was calling.

I let myself out of the guesthouse and answered the call.

"Uncle," I said, with warmth in my tone that I didn't feel. "How are you this morning? It's so nice to hear from you again so soon after our last call. Do you have good news for me?"

"No, I do not, niece," Grant said, and he sounded like a human pressure cooker about to pop. "I've been doing some light reading this morning, and I got bad news."

"Oh no," I said.

"Oh no, indeed, April. Just what were you thinking letting a person on board your truck?" he asked. "Have you lost your mind? Or would you prefer to go away to the farm, permanently?"

"Let's not get too hasty, Uncle." 'The farm' was a code phrase for going dark. It meant disappearing underground. It meant no more traveling on the food truck, no friends, no Hentie or Barkington. Heck, it meant sitting in a dark room with maybe a TV for company for extended periods of time.

Because I held secrets that were important to the NSIB, and if I was caught and tortured... Well, that simply couldn't happen.

"Are you trying to waste my money?" Grant asked.

He meant the department's funding.

"Do you know what a costly mistake you've made?" Grant asked.

Guilt sank through me like a stone sinking to the bottom of a pond. "I'm aware."

"You've already messed up twice. First with your old friend." *The Crown Prince.* "And second with your family."

It took great effort to remain in control. I wasn't a rookie, but thinking about Mickey and his passing was dangerous territory for me. He was the only person I'd met who had loved me for me. *Except, he didn't know the real you, did he? Only the version you allowed him to see.*

"Uncle, I assure you, everything's fine."

"Nothing is fine, April," he said. "You're treading a thin line, and you're one step from crossing over into dangerous territory."

"My friend is helping me keep that line," I said. "It's normal to have an assistant on a food truck."

"Not one that draws attention! Not one that—" Grant's breaths blew down the line. "This is close to a disaster. Trust me when I say this is going to be discussed at length in the family. There might be a review."

*Darn.* "Look, just give me a chance to get things under control, Uncle, all right? I promise, I can—"

"Absolutely not," Grant said. "Absolutely not. You're not to get anything under control, do you understand?"

"Uncle."

"My word is final, April. One more wrong step, and it's the farm for you."

"Anybody ever tell you you sound like Dr. Phil when you say stuff like that?"

But he'd already hung up, and it had been a lame joke anyway. I was in trouble. I should never have gotten involved with Hentie, and now she was in as much danger as I was.

*I'm not going to let her suffer the same consequences as Mickey.*

# Fifteen

I SPENT THE REST OF THE MORNING DISTRACTING myself from that phone call by serving ice cream on the truck. Hentie was a twitchy shadow of her former self who kept checking on Barkington in his crate every five minutes. He was a great emotional support to her, and it made me wish I had a dog of my own.

But the life of a spy on the run didn't lend itself to having a dog.

*Or friends, as Grant pointed out.*

The customers came in droves. People who leered at Hentie after the article in the newspaper this morning. It was just our luck that the newspaper had both an online and physical edition. There were a couple of people who sat on the bench that overlooked the bay, reading their papers, staring over the tops of them.

"All right," I said, at a quarter past one in the after-noon. "That's it for today."

"For the whole day?" Hentie asked. "But it's hot. The people will want ice creams."

"Then they can buy some store bought because I'm done with the staring. And you look like you're one ice cream cone away from passing out from fear."

"I'm fine. I promise."

"Hentie, it's okay. Let's clean up, grab Barkington, and go check out this jewelry store."

Hentie brushed her hands off on her cute pink and blue frilly apron. "That sounds like a plan."

The drive over to the jewelry store was taken in silence, with Barkington harnessed in his crate, and Hentie chewing on her nails and staring out at the passing brick stores. Once we were past the boardwalk, the streets quietened down a great deal.

The jewelry store was more of a boutique, and it wasn't a jewelry store that specialized in engagement rings or diamond necklaces. It was a specialty place, called Tink's Jewelry, with display cases that showed off rings, necklaces, and bracelets that had been hand-made. As indi-cated by the signs in the windows.

I opened the door and entered the well-lit shop, with its display cases and velvety blue wallpaper.

"Hello there." A woman smiled at us from the counter

at the front of the store. She wore a strange pair of binoculars that made her look steampunk and magnified her eyes by at least three times. She lifted them off her face and placed them atop her auburn curls. "My name's Tink. Pleasure to meet you."

"April," I said.

Hentie twitched. Barkington barked.

"This is Hentie and that's Barkington."

"Isn't he delightful," she said. "What an adorable dog. Cutest I've ever seen."

That got Hentie smiling back at the jeweler. "Do you want to pat him on the head?"

Tink wiped her hands off on her apron then circled her counter and offered Barkington a sniff of her fingers. He gave them a perfunctory lick and whined at her.

"What can I help you with today?" Tink asked. "Are you looking for a particular style of piece? I make tiaras and bracelets, rings, necklaces, just about anything you can think of, and I fill them with all my love and care."

"This is going to sound silly, but I'm a big fan of this ViewTube channel..." I trailed off, scanning the store and its shelves.

"Let me guess, Cressida's channel?" Tink asked.

"Yeah! You know her?"

"I knew her," Tink said. "She passed away recently."

"I heard," I said, lowering my head. "It's awful. I got

the opportunity to meet her once before *it* happened. She was a lovely woman."

"Was she?" Tink stopped petting Barkington and returned to the counter. "Sorry, that's me being snarky. Truth is, I didn't know her that well. I met her once when she came in here with her friend to order a pair of necklaces."

"Oh, you mean the one with the big red stone?" I asked. "The cursed necklace? She said she found that at Mary McClary's house."

"Ugh." Tink waved a hand and the bracelets on her arm tinkled and clacked. "That's a load of baloney. Ghosts and curses." She covered her mouth. "Sorry. You're a fan."

"Nah, that's okay," I said. "I'm a fan because it's fun, not because I necessarily believe it all. The whole reason I came here today was to find out if you could make me one of those necklaces."

"I sure can," Tink said. "I made two of them at the time, it should be easy enough to make another."

"Two, huh?" I asked.

Hentie had wandered off to another section of the store, probably because it was less pressure for her. I didn't blame her, and she didn't deserve the scrutiny she'd gotten. It wasn't her fault she'd come looking for us and stumbled upon a crime scene.

"Oh yeah, one for Cressida and one for her friend, uh... I can't remember her name?"

"Macy? Anne?"

"I'm not sure. I can't remember. She was wearing a hoodie, though. Can't remember much else about her." Tink waved a hand, bringing on another bout of bracelet clacking. "She was quiet. Kind of faded into the background, but, oh boy, was Cressida happy with the necklace. She basically told me what her plan was. But you won't want a necklace like hers anyway."

"What do you mean?"

"She asked me to drill a hole through the center of the garnet stone. The centerpiece of the necklace," Tink said, when I didn't immediately respond.

"A hole in the stone? What for?"

"No idea," she said, "but she wanted a hole in it. A small one."

"That's strange."

"Yeah," Tink said. "I thought so too. So, you want one?"

"How much does it cost?"

"These are handcrafted pieces, so they're not cheap. Like $500 if you collect it in the store."

My jaw dropped. Hentie made a choked noise from near a stand of rings, and we both looked over at her. "Listen, I've got a wealthy husband, and even that's too rich for my blood."

"Yeah," I said.

"Look, for a fan of Cressida, I can probably knock off fifty dollars, but that's the lowest I'm willing to go," Tink said, fluffing her hair. "What do you say?"

"You have a card?" I asked.

"Here." Tink handed me a white card that bore her name and contact number.

I tapped it against my index finger. "I'll think about it, okay? Thanks so much!"

"No problem. Call me if you need anything!"

Hentie and I left the store together while Tink waved at us. Once we were back inside the safety of the ice cream truck, Hentie turned to me. "Nee, man," she said. "That's far too expensive for a necklace."

"It's handcrafted," I said. "But this means that Cressida and her friend, we have to figure out who it was, dropped a thousand dollars on a pair of necklaces."

"Didn't you say that, uh, what's her face told you about the necklaces?"

"Macy," I said.

"That's the one."

"Yeah, she told me about this place. But that doesn't necessarily mean she was the one who bought the necklace with Cressida."

"Then it's got to be that Anne girl. I'm telling you, she's a stalker!"

Hentie didn't know what I did, and I couldn't let her in on the secret without revealing that I'd gone investigating without her. That and I had high-tech drone equipment that she couldn't know about as it would present a threat to national security.

"We have to do more digging before we can be sure," I said, and started the ice cream truck's engine.

<h1 style="text-align:center">Sixteen</h1>

Hentie had positioned herself in the armchair in my room at the guesthouse, Barkington in her lap, and a glass of iced tea on the coffee table and her phone in hand.

I had set up camp on my bed, my laptop in front of me. We were in full research mode. Anne was Hentie's target, and mine was Macy. I was suspicious of her, and Royson too. None of the suspects had been cleared, and the only thing working in Anne's favor at this point was that I hadn't seen her in the cemetery on the night of the murder.

But that didn't mean she wasn't there.

I found Macy's ViewTube channel easily. And the first video that popped up was a shocker.

"Hentie," I said. "You've got to see this." I got up and

went over to the sofa, settling into the comfy cushions and turning the laptop so she could see the screen.

Hentie leaned in to read the video's title and sucked in a breath.

**The truth about Cressida Keene...**

"She can't be serious," Hentie said. "Is that, uh, whatchamacallit? That thing that the ViewTubers do to get attention?"

"Clickbait?" I asked. "Looks like it. But what could she possibly have to say about Cressida? They're meant to be friends."

"With friends like that, who needs enemies, right? That's how that saying goes, isn't it?"

I hit play on the video.

Macy appeared on the screen. She was seated on the floor in what appeared to be her living room, in front of a brown leather sofa, and her eyes were filled with tears. She sniffled and wiped her fingers underneath either of them.

"Guys," she whispered. "I have to come clean."

The video immediately cut to a lengthy intro song that was reminiscent of something from the show *The X-Files*, except less cool.

She appeared back on screen. "Hey guys, I know this video will come as a shock to some of you, but after Cress's passing, I think it's important we have a heart to heart." She took a deep breath and shook her head. "The truth is,

Cressida, while she was my dear friend, wasn't who she claimed to be."

Hentie and I exchanged looks.

"This is bizarre," Hentie said.

I kept my thoughts to myself.

Macy brushed strands of dark hair back from her face. "I want to preface this by saying that Cressida was my dear friend. Like, my best friend. She was the one who invited me on her channel out of the goodness of her heart, and the way she... The way she passed? Nobody deserves that." A flood of tears followed the proclamation. "I can't believe I can't just call her up and talk to her."

When we'd met up with them in front of the cemetery, they hadn't seemed that close.

"You see," Macy said, "Cress was like a sister to me. She helped me set up my ViewTube channel, and honestly, I thought we were going to be friends forever. Like, we should have been. But going through this grieving process has helped me realize that some things have to come out into the open. There are secrets that aren't worth keeping, and this is one of them."

There was a moment of silence as Macy took a deep, dramatic breath.

"It all started when we first visited Mary McClary's house," Macy said. "You might recognize that name from one of my previous investigations. If you haven't seen that video, you can do so by clicking this link." She pointed up to her left and a video tab appeared.

"What is she up to?" Hentie asked.

Barkington barked.

"I remember I was super excited because it was my first time making a video with Cress, and she was so kind to me. We arrived at the house, and immediately, I could tell we were going to get some good stuff there. Like good footage. The house was super spooky, y'all. Like you wouldn't believe how creepy that house is." Another breath. "I was getting everything set up for recording when Cress invited another person into the house. The short of it is that she had someone there to make noises and move things. She had an entire set up to make her videos seem real. To make it seem like she was capturing EVPs and other phenomena when she wasn't."

Hentie gasped.

I was entirely unsurprised by the revelation. But, it was interesting that Macy had decided to reveal this on her channel. Not as interesting as the millions of views the video had gotten, though. It seemed that Macy's channel was doing *a lot* better now that Cressida wasn't around.

"You see, Cressida was faking her videos to get likes and views. I was in such disbelief that I didn't confront her about it immediately, and when I did, she told me that she didn't believe in ghosts. And that all of this stuff was fake, and surely I knew that. But the truth was I had captured real EVPs. When I told her that, she laughed at me. I wanted to be her friend so badly that I kept her secret, but now that she'd gone, I— It's just weighing heavy on my heart to keep this from all of you, especially since you've been so kind to me after her passing." She burst into tears again, between hiccups, Macy lifted her gaze to the camera. "I want you guys to know that Cress had her flaws, but she was a great person. Like, even though she faked that stuff and was a skeptic, she was so sweet and kind to me. Just go easy on her memory and on her family. They don't deserve hate, okay? I don't want my community to be a part of any hateful comments online. I'll see you in the next video." And then the video cut off abruptly.

"Dramatic," Hentie said.

I scrolled down to read some of the comments.

*User123344: I called it! I called it. I knew that Cressida was a huge fake.*

*Portsandshorts: You're so brave for coming out and saying this. Don't cry, oh my gosh.*

*Loieeebloeiii: Just another ViewTuber looking for atten-tion. Seriously? Get a real job!*

"This is getting a lot of attention," I said. "She's going to make money off this video. Ad revenue, that kind of thing."

"You think she killed Cressida for a video?" Hentie asked.

"Anything's possible, but it's not enough proof."

"Seems like nothing is enough proof," Hentie grumbled.

"On the plus side, at least the cops haven't come by to talk to you again, right?"

Hentie perked up. "Ja. But I could do without the news articles and all that stuff. People were staring at me on the truck today. Can I ask you something?"

"Sure."

"What do we do now? We know that Anne is suspicious and this ViewTuber girl too. But what's our next step?"

I thought about it for a second, shutting my laptop and placed it on the coffee table beside Hentie's iced tea. Barkington tilted his head, his collar rattling and clinking.

"We take the only logical step we have left."

"And that is?"

# Seventeen

There were several logical steps, but I couldn't tell Hentie about all of them, since she had no knowledge of my little fly drone or the pictures I'd taken. Regardless, the following morning, we piled into the ice cream truck together and drove out to our spot next to the boardwalk, overlooking the bay.

The early morning was cool, but the weather man had warned that today was going to be a "stinker."

Barkington had plenty of water in his crate, and Hentie and I had grabbed a filling breakfast. We were set for the day.

"So," Hentie said, "the plan."

"The plan."

"Yes, the plan. The wise and very easy to execute plan that you haven't told me anything about yet?"

"We're going to talk to Mr. Keene." I frowned, scratching my brow. "I told you that."

"Yeah, but what's the plan? Like, how? Where? What do we say?"

"It's best not to over complicate these things." I opened the side of the food truck, and we took our positions behind the rows of glistening domes that covered ice cream in every flavor. "But we'll take a break around lunch time to go talk to him. And we might let slip that Macy's channel is doing extra well now that Cressida has passed on."

"To anger him?"

"Not specifically," I said. "But he's been acting strange ever since his daughter's passing. I would say it's grief, but given his proximity to the crime scene…"

Hentie rubbed her palms together like an evil villain. "Ah yes. The *plan*."

I laughed, but the first customer arrived, and the line grew immediately. People loved ice cream in this town. Fair enough, it was summer, so they were bound to enjoy the stuff, but there was more to it than that.

There was an air of intrigue.

People stood in line and rose onto their tiptoes, craning their necks and trying to get a peek at the front of the truck. More specifically, at Hentie.

That article had drawn way too much attention to my friend, which made sleuthing difficult. But Hentie managed to serve each customer with a smile, eye twitches and all.

We were about to close the truck after lunch for a quick break and to execute "the plan", as Hentie liked to put it, when a familiar face appeared at the front of the line.

Cookie, from the bakery, sniffed that prominent nose. "April," she said. "That's your name, right?"

"Yeah," I said, "we met the other day. What can I get for you today, Cookie? We've got loads of flavors." I gestured to the steel ice cream containers. Little signs poked out of the ice cream, designating their flavors, from Mint Freeze to Caramel Drip, with its swirls of gooey caramel through vanilla ice cream.

Cookie studied the selection then glanced at the chalk-board behind our heads that displayed the prices. "I'll take one scoop of Mint Freeze and one of the chocolate."

"Excellent choice," I said. "Sugar cone or cup?"

"Cup, please."

I smiled at Cookie and scooped out her order into a cute pink and blue cup bearing the truck's name then handed it over. She took a bite of the ice cream before paying, but didn't immediately leave.

"Can I get something else for you?" I asked, as Hentie served another customer beside me.

"Have you seen Anne?" Cookie asked.

"No," I said. "I haven't. Why?"

"She didn't show up for work yesterday," she said. "Or this morning. And I need her to show up so that I can fire her for her utter negligence."

"Oh, wow. No, sorry, I don't know where she is."

Cookie let out a sigh. "It's so difficult to find trustworthy staff nowadays. You know, this was her final strike. It's not like I didn't try to make an effort with her. She refused to fall into line. She kept breaking the rules."

"How?" I asked.

Cookie leaned in, taking another bite of ice cream with her paddle spoon. "She allowed pets in the bakery, which is strictly against the rules, because some of my staff are allergic. I can't put people in danger."

"That's—"

"And," Cookie continued, waving her spoon around, flinging flecks of ice cream to the ground, "she liked to bring her boyfriend to the bakery after closing time. I had to take her key away. She was in line to be the manager at one point. Entrusting her with a key to the bakery was the worst decision I ever made hands down. Dubbah."

"Wow, I had no idea."

"Why would you?" Cookie asked, and took another bite of ice cream. "This is delicious, by the way."

"Thank—"

"And you know what makes it even worse?" Cookie sniffed. "There were rumors about her after that woman died the other day. You know that, uh, ViewTubing girl. The one who liked the ghosts? I heard my staff gossiping about the fact that Anne might've been the one to do it."

"Why would they think that?"

"Because she was practically obsessed with the girl."

Hentie coughed beside me and it sounded suspiciously like the words, "Told you so."

"And I was the one who stood up for Anne," Cookie said. "That's the problem with being an empath like me. People just walk all over you, especially when you're a people-pleaser."

"That's kind of you to stand up for—"

"I know. I know. I'm so kind. *So kind.*"

"En heeltemal nederig," Hentie said.

"What did she say?" Cookie asked.

Hentie motioned beside her lip, a key turning in a lock.

"Uh, I don't know, but you were saying that—"

"Ayuh." Cookie swept hair from her forehead. "I was so kind to that girl. Oh gosh, it makes me emotional the way I got taken advantage of, but here we are. I give, and I give, and I give. Even when the police showed up asking questions, I was the one who stood up for her. I told them that she was at the bakery on the night of the murder."

"Was she?" Hentie and I asked, in unison.

"She was there with her boyfriend," Cookie said. "I had to come drag her out of there and give her another *warning* for breaking the rules. I took the key away from her, of course, because how could I possibly trust her after that?"

"Of course, you wouldn't be—"

"I couldn't. I couldn't trust her. And now, she's broken my trust again." There were a couple of other customers left in the line, and they were listening in, reacting to every word from Cookie. It was clear the bakery owner wanted an audience. A pity party.

But it worked in our favor.

Cookie sniffled away from the truck once she'd gotten her dose of attention.

*Not as enraged today, so there's that.* I looked over at Hentie, who raised both gray eyebrows at me. Anne was gone? Anne, our stalker suspect, was missing. There was food for thought. And she had an alibi.

If that was true, why was she gone? Why hadn't she turned up at work?

We served the last of the customers in line, then closed

up the side of the truck, checked on Barkington, and started our drive over to the Keene's place.

If anyone would be able to answer our questions, it was Royson. Those pictures in Anne's house had told me as much.

*Eighteen*

"I'M KIND OF IN THE MIDDLE OF SOMETHING," Royson said, straightening his apron. "I'm cooking dinner for Mama." He held the door open, and the scents of cooking drifted out of his home. He had a fancy house overlooking the bay—prime real estate—with floor-to-ceiling windows and a front hall that was filled with potted plants.

Sam had given us the address, but the place was hard to miss. It was built against Carmel Springs' only hill, and it stood out, a white and glass monstrosity against the green of the trees that surrounded it.

"We wanted to stop by and check in on how you were doing," I said.

Hentie held Barkington, who gave a bark.

"Everyone in this town is so darn nosy," Royson said.

"I haven't had a moment's peace since Cress passed. Not a single moment to myself, and I have responsibilities too. It's not like I'm lazing around. I have a funeral to organize, a mother to look after, and I don't even have time to grieve for my daughter."

Hentie's jaw had dropped.

"Why would I want either of you in my house?" Royson asked, eyes narrowing. "You were both there. You were the ones who found Cress's body, and you..." He pointed at Hentie. "You're the prime suspect. No, I don't want you here. Leave."

"Mr. Keene," I said. "We're not trying to upset you, but there's something you should know. Two things. It's about Cressida's ViewTube channel."

He had been seconds away from slamming the door in our faces, but he paused. "What about it?"

"You haven't been keeping an eye on it, have you?" I asked.

"What? What are you talking about? I was Cressida's editor. I'm the one in charge of making sure everything is scheduled and uploaded on time. Of course, I'm keeping an eye on it."

I brought my phone out of my pocket and showed him the screen.

I'd had a feeling he wouldn't want to talk to us and that this man worshiped that channel above anything else.

"What's this?" Royson took my phone and scrolled through the comments on the screen.

"The comments on Cressida's last video," I said. "They're all negative."

"I can see that," Royson whispered. "What on earth?"

"If you want answers, I can tell you why this is happening," I said.

Royson hesitated. He handed me back my phone. "Fine. Fine, you can come in, but you better make this quick. Mama is hungry." He gestured for us to enter.

We followed him down the broad, wooden hallway and into a living room with a cozy fireplace, unlit, and a view of the bay far below. An elderly woman sat in a wheelchair in front of the windows in the sun. A ginger cat was curled up in her lap. It opened one eye and studied Barkington with suspicion.

Hentie and Barkington sat on a leather sofa while I remained standing, my hands tucked behind my back.

"Hello," I said, merrily.

"Don't bother." Royson waved a hand. "She doesn't talk. She hasn't for years now."

"Oh. But surely we can still say hello."

Royson rolled his eyes. "Mama, I'm getting these guests some lemonade. I'll be right back." And then he strode out of the room, stiff as a board.

Hentie pulled a face and opened her mouth, but

snapped it shut again when the woman wheeled her chair around with a sense of urgency. She zoomed over to us and stopped, leaning forward.

"Be careful," she whispered, her voice raspy.

Hentie and I both jumped. Barkington let out a yap, and Hentie covered his little snout. The cat in the woman's lap leaped away and hightailed it out of the room.

"There's a lot you don't know," Mama said. "There's a lot he won't tell you."

"What do you mean?" I whispered.

"He forced Cressida to make those videos. She didn't want to make them. She didn't—"

Footsteps sounded in the hall, and Mama wheeled her chair away, back to the spot she'd been in before.

Both Hentie and I were stunned. I snapped an image of Mama for my corkboard, and watched as a thin red line connected her back to Cressida's body, and to the image I had taken of Anne, Royson, and Mama together.

What *exactly* was going on in this family?

Royson entered with a tray of tall glasses filled with ice and cloudy lemonade, setting it down on the coffee table.

"Now," he said, "you owe me an explanation."

"Macy made a video about Cressida," I said, "claiming that she never believed in ghosts, and that her entire channel was a lie."

"What?" Royson's expression darkened. "What did you say?"

"It's true." I lifted my phone out of my lap and tapped through to the video in question. "This is the video. You can take a look for yourself once we're gone. I thought you ought to know."

"That little witch," Royson said. "She's such a liar. Cressida gave everything for this channel, and she dares question her? After Cress insisted that we invite her on this ghost tour. I told her this was a terrible idea, and she wouldn't listen. She wanted Macy there. I'm going to find that girl and make her pay." That last sentence was said through gritted teeth.

"There's more, Mr. Keene," I said.

"How can there be *more*?" Royson asked. "Hasn't my family been through enough? This town already hates us because of how popular we are."

*We? More like Cressida.* A power hungry father who may have killed his daughter for attention? Because he didn't agree with her creative choices?

A tenuous line spread from the picture of the back-pack stash in Mary McClary's house to Cressida's body. Was it hers? Or was it Anne's? Anne had an alibi provided by a woman who didn't even like her very much, so she couldn't be the murderer.

I blinked and focused on Royson. "Anne's missing."

"Who's Anne?" Royson asked.

*Liar, liar.* "Anne, Cressida's friend? I think she may have bought a necklace with her? Like a friendship necklace?" That was a wild guess. We still weren't sure if Cressida and Macy had bought necklaces together, or if it had been Cress and Anne.

"I have no idea who you're talking about."

"Anne," I said. "She works at Cookie's Cupcakery? Blonde hair, young, friendly. Likes pets."

Royson shrugged. "Sorry. Doesn't ring a bell."

He couldn't be serious. That was a blatant lie, and he had no reason to lie about Anne. Or did he? "Either way, she's missing, and, uh, it might be connected to what happened to Cressida."

Royson stiffened. "Oh, well then, in that case, I advise you to report it to the police. I can't help you with that." And then he nodded toward the door.

Hentie rose and started toward the exit. On our way out, I cast one last glance toward Mama, who sat with her hands in her lap. "It was him," she mouthed.

Royson looked over at her, and she put on a hazy stare. He frowned for a moment then shook his head and guided us out.

"Thanks for the hospitality, Mr. Keene."

The door slammed behind us without a reply.

# Nineteen

"That was crazy," Hentie said, as we drove back toward the Oceanside. "I can't believe what that old tannie said."

"Tannie?"

"It's like an old lady." Hentie peered out of the window as we drove past the ocean and the boardwalk, packed with happy tourists and locals, shopping or eating, or having a great time. "Anyways, I can't believe that. That guy thinks she doesn't talk, meanwhile she's ready to rat him out for being a bad father."

"Huh," I said. "It's definitely interesting." I pressed my foot onto the brake pedal at an intersection, frowning.

My mind wouldn't stop, a common thing for me, and connections formed and broke repeatedly as I worked over the problem.

*Anne missing?*

*Father is a liar.*

*Macy's benefitting.*

But if Anne had an alibi, surely that meant it could only be one of the two of them, unless there was another person who'd been around? And what about the necklace? The hole in the necklace specifically.

We had to find it.

The murderer must have taken it.

But what if they hadn't taken it with them, but had ripped it off and disposed of it instead?

I put on my indicator and turned right, heading away from the seaside and into the suburbs.

"And now?" Hentie asked, smoothing her hands over her baby blue pants suit. "Where are we going?"

"To Berry Lane," I said. "I want to see if Anne's home. There's something strange going on. Why didn't she show up at work? What is she hiding?"

"Maybe she's in danger. What if Royson kidnapped her because she knows something?"

I didn't answer. It was possible that Royson had done something to Anne, but there was no evidence yet.

The house on Berry Lane was silent. I knocked on the cute colorful front door while Hentie waited in the ice cream truck. Nothing. No answer. And a quick peek through the windows showed me the TV was off and the interior was silent.

I was on my way back to the truck when my phone trilled in my pocket.

I stopped and withdrew it. A foreign number flashed on the screen.

Impossible.

Grant was the only one who had this number. And he would *never* give it out to anyone else.

I'd been so fixated on this case, I'd completely set aside the fact that there were people after me. People who wanted me dead.

I stared at the flashing number on the screen until it fell silent. And then it started up again.

If I answered this and talked to whoever was on the other end of the line for too long, they'd be able to trace the call. It was safer to dump the phone and buy a new one, upload Grant's number and call him to tell him it had been compromised.

*And then he'll make you go dark.*

Darn. Why was everything so messy?

I waited for the call to cancel then put my phone on silent and joined Hentie in the truck.

"She's not in there?" Hentie asked.

"No. She's not. But I think I know where she might be," I said.

WE PARKED THE TRUCK OUTSIDE MARY McClary's house then walked around the outside of it, as we'd done the last time we'd been here. The afternoon had worn on, and the light was dim underneath the trees that surrounded the spooky old house.

Hentie held Barkington as we picked our way toward the back gate. "It's so quiet," Hentie said.

And she was right. It had gone silent in the past few seconds, almost as if the trees themselves were holding their breath.

I crept toward the fence. A scuffling noise came from behind the brick barrier wall, and I waved at Hentie to back up.

She stepped back onto a twig, the *snap* echoing through the quiet.

*Darn.*

The shuffling stopped. There was another moment of that gravid silence, and then—

"Who's out there?" A man called.

I waved again and pointed for Hentie to head back toward the truck. I recognized that voice. It belonged to...

The gate creaked open and Detective White walked around the corner. The noise in the woods resumed, but the tension remained. White sighed and stroked a palm over his bald head. "What are you two doing here?"

"Hi Detective," I said, with a smile. "How are you?"

Hentie had gone quiet and into full "eye twitch" mode. I stepped between her and the detective, hoping to distract from how freaked out she was by his presence.

"She good?" White asked, removing a stick of gum from his pocket. He inserted it between his lips and started chewing. "I'd offer you some, but it's to help me quit smoking." He patted his top pocket.

"Good for you, Detective," I said.

"You haven't answered my question. Slippery as always, Miss Waters."

"Sorry," I said. "I'm not trying to withhold anything from you. You took us by surprise."

"And why's that?"

"We didn't expect anyone to be here," I said, and looked down at my feet. "Oh gosh, it's silly but we've been on a ghost hunting kick ever since we took a tour at the cemetery."

"You're referring to the tour where a woman died?" White asked.

"Unfortunately, yeah," I said. "But that's not really what got us into ghost hunting."

He chewed furiously, his eyes flickering to the left. I

turned and spotted Hentie making a hasty retreat toward the truck.

"What's her deal?"

"She's stressed," I said. "Being accused of murder will do that to a woman."

"Yeah, about that," Detective White said. "Sorry. The editor of the local paper got a hold of the story and ran with it. We haven't officially released a statement yet, so you can tell your friend to relax."

"Can I?"

Detective White went quiet again.

That quiet stretched, and stretched, and stretched, and finally, *snapped*.

"So you're ghost hunting. That's all," White said.

"That's all," I said. "Just an innocent little ghost hunt."

"And you expect me to believe that you're *here*, ghost hunting."

"I don't understand, Detective," I laughed. "What's wrong with us being here?"

"You're trespassing." But there was obviously more to it than that. Was the detective looking for Anne too? Had he not found her here?

"Technically, we didn't go inside," I said. "So are we really trespassing?"

White chewed some more. He took a step toward me.

"Look, April, I like you. You've got backbone. And that's why I'm gonna do you a favor here, and tell you to turn around, walk away, get in your truck, and keep your nose out of my case."

"No idea what you mean, Detective. I haven't done anything."

"Sure, you haven't. Sure."

I offered him another winning smile. I hoped. "I'll see you around town, Detective. You should stop by the truck some time for ice cream. You got a favorite flavor?"

"Justice," he said.

"They should put that on a t-shirt." And then I turned around and made for the truck.

*Darn, darn, darn.* How were we supposed to find Anne if we couldn't visit what was clearly her old haunt. If both Anne and Cressida had hung out here, could this be their meeting place? Anne had said it was her spot, but now we didn't have access.

Hentie gave me a look that was all wobbly chin when I got into the car.

"Don't worry," I said, patting her knee. "He doesn't suspect a thing."

I started the truck and directed us back toward the center of town. I didn't care what Detective White wanted. We were going to find Anne today.

# Twenty

"WHERE ARE WE GOING?" HENTIE ASKED, ONCE we hit Main Street.

"Cookie's Cupcakery," I said. "I want to ask Cookie about Anne's boyfriend. If she's not at home and she's not at Mary McClary's house, then this guy has to know where she's gone."

"Should we report it to the cops?" Hentie asked. "If she's missing?"

"Hmm. If we don't find her after we've checked in with the boyfriend, then yes." I had full confidence in my ability to find her because of my training. If I had to drop Hentie off at the Oceanside and do this by myself, I would.

I parked the ice cream truck in front of Cookie's Cupcakery and turned to Hentie, but she was frozen in shock, her mouth wide open.

"Hentie?" I patted her on the arm. "Hentie? What's wrong? Hello?"

"Kyk! I mean, look. Look!" She lifted a finger, pointing out of the front of the truck.

There was nothing on the sidewalk. What on earth was she—?

*Oh.*

The commotion was taking place *inside* the bakery. Royson Keene held a box of cupcakes. He held one in his hand, and he was screaming so hard, his entire face was red. Macy stood in front of him with her phone out, recording him as he had his meltdown.

"What the—?" I got out of the car and jogged up to the door.

I entered and a wall of sound hit me.

"—think I don't know what you've been planning?" Royson shouted the question. "You're trying to destroy Cressida's channel."

"As you can see, this guy is absolutely losing his mind. This is Cressida's father, and he's the one who's been controlling her channel," Macy said matter-of-factly.

In the background, the servers were stunlocked. Every customer in the place stared at the ongoing altercation. Where was Cookie? She would put a stop to this for sure.

"You're a little liar. I never controlled Cressida. She

wanted to do this. She wanted to be famous, and she was but you made sure that her name was besmirched! You'd better watch your back, little girl."

"Or what, Mr. Keene?" Macy asked, lifting one shoulder. She wore a pair of black ripped tights and a striped shirt, and she looked empowered. Like she was ready to kick butt. "What are you going to do? Kill me?"

A gasp rippled through the bakery.

Royson narrowed his eyes. "You're evil. You're messing with my livelihood."

"Oh, so you're worried about what will happen to Cressida's money, is that right?" Macy asked. "It's her money, isn't it? Since she's the one who made the videos." She waved the phone toward him.

"Get that out of my face," he snarled, and pushed her hand back. Then, he lifted the cupcake and rammed it toward her.

Macy dodged back before it hit home, and the crowd gasped. "Did everyone see that? He just tried to assault me. You're on camera, Mr. Keene! Everyone saw what you did."

But it didn't look like he was going to stop. He took another cupcake and threw it at her.

*This has to be stopped.*

The door opened behind me, and Hentie and Barkington came inside. Immediately, Barkington started yipping and squirming, clearly distressed about what was taking place right in front of us.

"Enough," I said.

But neither of them listened to me.

Macy continued jeering and recording. Royson reached for her hand and grabbed hold of her wrist.

*Unacceptable.*

I walked past Royson then reached up and pinched the back of his elbow. Royson's fingers released instantly, and Macy stumbled back, lifting her phone again. Royson rounded on me, his glare hot and full of anger.

I leveled him with the stare that my family was known for. The Mission stare that turned men's legs to jelly and struck fear into his heart.

Royson took a single step forward before he noticed the look on my face.

"Try me," I whispered.

He swept his gaze over me then frowned and sniffed. He didn't move a muscle. Didn't yell.

"Just what in the world is going on out here?" The thunderous shout came from the swinging kitchen doors. Cookie strode into the bakery, stripping off a pair of oven mitts as she walked. "Who is shouting in my bakery?"

"He threw cupcakes at me," Macy said. "He grabbed my arm. I demand you throw him out of here."

There were cupcakes littered across the floor, crumbs and clumps of buttercream frosting.

"She's a witch," Royson said. "You mark my words. She's the one responsible for all of this. She wanted to get rid of my daughter. She's evil!"

"The only evil one in this town is you, Mr. Keene," Macy replied.

"Both of you stop clucking like hens laying eggs," Cookie snapped, placing her fists on her hips, "and get out of my bakery. Now."

"Me?" Macy gestured to her chest in disbelief. "But I—"

"Now." Cookie pointed toward the door, and at the same time, her eagle-eyed gaze landed on Hentie and Barkington. "No pets allowed."

Hentie didn't need to be told twice this time.

"All right," Cookie said, after the door had swung shut behind them. "Now, I suggest the rest of you enjoy your baked goods in peaceful quiet before I throw all of you out and close down for the day. Nancy? Nancy! Would you get out here and clean this up, please? I've got a dozen cupcakes in the oven."

"Coming, Miss Cookie!" A scrawny teenager appeared from behind the counter, scuttling to do as she was told.

Cookie huffed and started toward the kitchen, but I tapped her on the shoulder before she got too far.

"What's up?" She frowned at me.

"Sorry to bother you, Cookie."

"Bother me? Only thing that bothers me is that couple of dubbahs acting the fool."

"I take it you're right out straight?"

Cookie flashed me a grin. "Ah, you're learning," she said. "Ayuh, I certainly am. What do you want, dear?"

"Anne's boyfriend," I said. "What's his name?"

"Cory Willis," she replied, with a wave of her hand. "Works down at the grocery store on the corner as a cashier. A couple of apples short of a pie, if you ask me, but he's not a bad kid. Why?"

"You mentioned Anne hadn't come into work. I figured her boyfriend might know where she'd gone."

"Good thinking," Cookie said. "If you find her, do me a favor and give her a kick up the behind. That girl has given me about five extra gray hairs from her shenanigans." And then she swept toward the kitchen doors and disappeared inside.

I exited into the fading light. The bakery would close its doors soon enough, and who knew how late the grocery store would stay open. "I got his name," I said, through the open window on Hentie's side of the truck.

Barkington had his little Chihuahua paws perched on the window sill. I stroked his head.

"Want to come with me?" I asked. "It's just a walk down the street."

"I would," Hentie said, "but, ja, I don't know if my heart can handle it."

Twenty-One

I WALKED DOWN THE STREET ON MY OWN, PHONE in hand, my gaze focused on the corner up ahead. Casually, without missing a step, I switched off my phone then tossed it into a trash can I passed by. If I was being tracked by that strange caller, I had to get rid of it. I'd buy another one online and have it shipped to me if there wasn't a tech store in town. I'd already backed up any pictures I'd taken to my laptop.

The grocery store on the corner was lit up inside, showing off displays of vegetables and canned goods, with three cashiers waiting at checkout stations. I opened the glass front door and walked over to the only male cashier.

Short and with bony elbows and an oversized smock, he wore a pair of glasses that sat on the tip of his nose. Had to be in his twenties. I took a mental snapshot of him and filed it away to be added to the corkboard if necessary.

"Hi," I said, "you're Anne's boyfriend, Cory, right?"

"Ayuh. And you are?"

"I'm a friend," I said. "Anne didn't show up for work yesterday or this morning. Do you have any idea where she might be?"

Cory went pale and pressed his lips into a tight, thin line.

"It's very important you tell me where she is," I said. "I think she might be in danger, and I'm trying to help her."

"Are you a cop?" he asked, whispering it, and giving the cashier at the next stand a healthy dose of side-eye.

Whenever I was asked this question, there was only one right answer depending on the person.

"No," I said. "I'm not."

He nodded. "You're her friend? I've never seen you around before?"

"I work on the ice cream truck. Anne mentioned that she'd been having trouble at work. She said that Cookie threw cupcakes at her." And then it hit me, right between the eyes. A rush of images affronted me, a soft whirring in my brain that was audible to me and no one else.

Anne crying, her shirt stained red from food coloring we'd thought was blood. Her claiming that it had been Cookie who'd plastered her with cupcakes.

And then this afternoon's snapshot of Mr. Keene throwing cupcakes at Macy, grabbing hold of her arm.

The warning from Mama about Royson being dangerous.

But that blurry image on my corkboard wasn't completely clear.

Regardless, I had to find Anne. She had an answer to this, I was sure of it, and she definitely wasn't the killer since she'd been with Cory at the time of the murder.

"—you okay?" Cory's words reached my ears.

My head snapped up. "Yeah. Fine. Sorry, I, uh, I have a condition. Anyway, where is Anne? This is super important. I tried Mary McClary's house and her place, but I can't find her."

"This is going to sound really weird," Cory whispered. "But Anne's been acting different lately. She's always been into alternative stuff, you know? Like different kinds of music, and even horror movies, and stuff I'm not into. But that's whatever. Lately, she's been even more into that stuff. She asked me to drop her off at the cemetery."

"And you did? When?"

"This afternoon," he said. "She said it was important and that it would help bring Cressida's killer to justice."

"Was Anne close with her?"

Another sideways glance at the other cashiers. The

fluorescent lights buzzed overhead, a sound that burrowed into my thoughts in the quiet.

"Cory?"

"I don't know," he said. "She mentioned they were friends in high school and that they kind of drifted apart afterward. I don't know what happened, but she's been torn up about Cressida's death. I don't know why, or what she's got to do with any of this, but it's kind of freaking me out." Cory blew out a breath. "Honestly, it's a relief to talk to somebody about it."

"Thanks, Cory," I said. "Thanks for trusting me. I've got to talk to Anne. I'll make sure she's safe." And then I spun on my heel and headed back out of the doors.

Anne had gone to the cemetery. She'd returned to the scene of the crime. Why? Why go back? And did she have the necklace? What was she trying to prove? She couldn't be the killer, unless Cory had helped her falsify her alibi and the pair of them had murdered Cressida?

But we'd have seen them there.

The picture was still foggy. What was it?

I reached up and gripped my head shaking it, as I approached the ice cream truck. My footsteps stalled.

Two men in black suits stood beside the passenger side door talking to Hentie. The one wore a pair of sunglasses. The other didn't. They held briefcases, and they were both nondescript. The type of guys who could pass for anybody in a pinch.

*Agents.*

Looking for me?

Had to be.

And that would explain the call from earlier—the unknown number. Darn it, I should have gotten rid of that phone sooner. They obviously traced it.

I dipped into an alleyway between a bookstore and a clothing boutique and watched them talking to Hentie. She didn't seem uncomfortable, but if these men were professionals, she wouldn't be uncomfortable right up until the point they snapped her neck.

*Ooh, don't go there.* The thought of Hentie or Barkington in danger made my pulse race.

Regardless, I kept my breathing even and studied them.

They talked to her for a couple of minutes longer, the second guy lighting up a cigarette and looking up and down the street. I kept out of sight.

At last, the men moved off. They got into a black sedan together, red tail lights bright in the dusk. I counted to ten then stepped out of the alleyway and started up the street. I got into the ice cream truck, put on my seatbelt, and started the engine.

"Oh, hey, wag 'n bietjie," Hentie said, then clicked her tongue. "I mean, wait. I have to put Barkington in his harness."

"We need to get out of here now. Hold onto him. I'll stop down the road and you can put him in the harness."

"But—"

I wasn't about to take chances. Those guys could circle back any second. I took off down the street, took a couple of corners, then parked on the side of the road so that Hentie could strap Barkington into his crate harness.

"What's going on here?" Hentie asked. "You came back to the truck and started acting like a different person."

"Who were those men you were talking to?"

"I don't know," Hentie said. "Just some guys. They asked if the truck will be open tomorrow and where they can find us."

"And you told them," I said.

"Of course. They were potential customers. Friendly guys," Hentie said. "April, what's the matter?"

"Nothing, Hentie. We've got to get to the cemetery. Anne's there, and I think she has all the answers to our questions." At least the ones related to the murder case.

The men and the mysterious call were another story.

One thing was for sure, I wasn't going to park the

truck next to the boardwalk tomorrow. Unless it was to trap these guys and take them down before they could get to me.

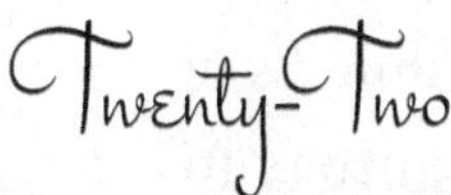

HENTIE PLACED BARKINGTON ON THE END OF A leash next to the truck while I locked up and studied the gates to the cemetery. They were still open, though the sun had officially set. How much longer would they stay that way?

I was happy to scale a wall to get out, but I doubted Hentie would be willing or able to, especially with Barkington.

"Ready!" Hentie declared.

Barkington barked and tugged on the end of his lead. He didn't usually wear one, but it was dark, and the last time we'd come to the cemetery, he'd run off.

"All right," I said. "We'll make this as quick as we can. Stay aware, and if you see something, say something. Got it?"

"Got it."

"Also, no barking," I said.

Barkington wagged his tiny tail.

"And no screaming."

Hentie gave me a thumbs up.

We entered the cemetery together. I hadn't kept track of how the police investigation had gone, but there were no police lines, which likely meant that they were done collecting evidence. And that the cemetery was open to the public again.

The quiet between the graves was ominous. I kept my eyes peeled for any sign of Anne, but there was nothing obvious.

"Should we split up?" Hentie asked.

My gut said no, so I shook my head.

We continued on the path, Barkington pattering along, his little collar tinkling as he went. Occasionally, he stopped to sniff a bush or raise his leg, and Hentie would click her tongue at him, but wait for him patiently.

"The treeline," I whispered. "Let's go."

Clearly, Anne wasn't hanging out in the main portion of the cemetery. Had she returned to the scene of the crime? The old church? If that was true, why?

She was involved with the family. Keene had thrown cupcakes at her, I was certain of that, but why?

Our trio moved through the trees together, and when

the going got rough, Hentie lifted Barkington into her arms and held him close. I didn't have my phone for a flashlight, and the night was quiet.

Hentie brought her phone out and we used its light to navigate the weeds and trees. Rustling in the undergrowth set me on edge, but there were no footsteps. When we were close to the crime scene, I took the phone from Hentie and covered the light.

"She could be here," I whispered. "We have to be careful."

"What's that?" Hentie asked. "Do you hear that or am I going crazy?" Barkington growled, an adorable noise from such a tiny dog.

I held a finger to my lips, and we both went quiet.

And then I heard it. The rough crunch of a shovel hitting dirt. Someone was digging in the cemetery.

Hentie's jaw dropped. "A sh-sh-sh-shovel," she whispered.

"It's okay," I said. "You stay here with Barkington."

"Are you joking?" Hentie asked. "I must stay here in the dark alone?"

I handed her the phone. "Don't worry. I'll be quick. If you hear me call for help, get the cops on the line."

"Be careful, April."

"I'll be fine," I said, and patted her arm. "Don't stress."

And then I crept toward the ruins of the old church.

As far as I knew, there weren't any gravestones among the ruins. Rubble marred the grass, and there were the old jagged lines and stubs of the church walls, weeds growing from between the stones, but no graves. Clouds drifted across the inky sky, and the moon, which was waxing, cast light on the ground, helping me navigate in utter quiet.

A figure appeared near the opposite side of the clearing, between the stones. The moonlight glinted on blonde hair.

Anne leaned on her shovel, wiping sweat off her brow. "Darn," she muttered. "Where is it? I swear I marked it with the stones."

I didn't say a word, creeping closer still.

She hefted the shovel and bit the sharp end into the dirt again. She tossed dirt off to one side, digging like a woman possessed until finally, there was a metallic clank. "Ah! Got it."

Anne bent and fumbled in the ground in front of her, swiping her fingers through the dirt. She grunted and heaved a small metal container out of the ground then placed it in front of her.

*Easy. Don't do anything yet.*

I took a mental picture of her, crouched over the box, her hands on either side of it, holding it like it was incredibly precious to her.

Anne unlatched the box and opened the lid. The

moonlight glinted off the red stone inside, and she let out a breath. "There you are," she whispered. "Thank goodness."

"Hi Anne," I said.

She let out a horrified scream that echoed through the ruins.

Barkington yipped and howled from underneath the trees, and Hentie appeared, jogging toward us, her gray bun bobbing. "What happened? Are you okay?"

"Nothing yet," I said.

Anne stared up at us like a deer caught in headlights, and Hentie lifted the flashlight beam and directed it at her.

"Anne," I said, "fancy meeting you out here. What are you doing?"

She gulped.

"I think she's frozen in fear," Hentie said helpfully, and Barkington barked his agreement.

"Anne?" I reached for her.

She let out a squawk then grabbed the necklace out of the box, tucked it into her shirt, and leaped up. Anne sprinted toward the treeline, heading away from the entrance to the cemetery rather than toward it.

"Darn," I muttered.

"Get her!" Hentie cried and started trampling through the ruins.

I admired the enthusiasm as I set off after our target.

Anne darted between the trees, nimble, and definitely younger than me. I followed close on her heels, gaining on her in the dark, leaping over stones and roots where I could see them, stumbling here or there.

My arms and legs burned as we headed deeper into the trees. Anne took plenty of turns left and right, panting as she ran. She cast glances over her shoulder, letting out a squeal when she realized how close I was to catching her.

"Give it up, Anne!" I called. "We're not here to hurt you. We're here to help."

But she either didn't hear me or didn't believe us, because she didn't stop. She took a sharp left and ran into a tree with a meaty crunch. Anne stumbled back and fell on her butt in the dirt, groaning and gripping her face.

I dropped down beside her, my heart racing. "Are you okay?"

Anne scrambled to get up, but I grabbed hold of her arm and held her there. "Hey, calm down. I'm not going to hurt you."

Anne yelled and squirmed.

"Stop!"

Hentie's footsteps thundered through the woods and light flooded the scene. She blew out a breath. "That's my exercise for the year." Barkington whined.

Anne tried to run again, and I pulled her back down.

Her nose was bleeding, and her eyes were watery with unshed tears. "Let me go," she howled.

"Anne, stop it. I know you didn't kill Cressida. I'm here to help. We're here to help."

Hentie leaned against a tree to catch her breath. She nodded. "Ja. What she said."

"Help?" Anne whispered it into the night.

"Yeah," I said. "Help. But we can't help you if you don't tell us what's going on. I'm going to let go of you now, okay? Don't run."

I released her, and Anne massaged her arm like I'd taken her out of cuffs.

Hentie fished tissues out of her pants suit pocket and handed them over to Anne, who dabbed at her nose.

"Are you okay?" Hentie asked.

"I'm fine," she said. "I don't think it's broken. I just smashed it against that tree."

And then there was silence while she stared up at us, bewildered, even a little questioning.

"We know that you didn't murder Cressida," I said. "And that it wasn't Cookie who threw those cupcakes at you. So why don't you tell us what you're doing out here, and why you just dug up Cressida's necklace."

"How do you know all this stuff?" Anne asked, removing the necklace from her camisole top. She clasped it in her palm, closing her fingers around it.

"Because everyone in this town thinks my friend committed the murder," I said, gesturing over my shoulder toward Hentie. "And she definitely *did* not. So, we've been asking some questions, figuring stuff out, that kind of thing."

"Ja."

Barkington yipped as well.

It was nice to have back up. It was kind of funny too—that image of Hentie jogging through the ruins would be stuck in my mind forever.

"What's going on, Anne?"

She swallowed, opening her palm to look at the shimmering necklace. Hentie directed the beam toward it, and I caught sight of the stone, and the small depression at its center.

"I don't know where to start," Anne said. "It's complicated."

"Why don't you start by telling us about your relationship with Cressida?"

"We were friends. Best friends," she said. "For a really, really long time. Until she started up this ghost hunting channel. Actually, that's not true. It was her dad who made her start the channel. Cressida didn't even believe in ghosts. She didn't want to be a part of it, but her dad made her. He was super controlling and just a bad guy to her. He told her what she could wear, eat, do, it was over the top, and I couldn't stand it."

"I'm sorry," I said.

"Yeah, at the start of the channel, it wasn't so bad, but once it started really taking off, he was a tyrant. He wouldn't let her come out and chill or hang with her friends." Anne sniffed and cleared her throat. "And when I brought it up to her, she was kind of afraid to talk about it. But slowly, over time, she gathered her courage and stood up to him. That was when he banned me from seeing her."

"Oh my gosh," Hentie said, and set Barkington down.

The pup, sensing Anne's distress, ran over and clambered into her lap. She stroked him and he whined and wagged his butt.

"But I wasn't about to let him get away with that," Anne said. "So we came up with a plan. We promised to meet up at Mary McClary's house every Sunday. We started gathering a stash of stuff. Getaway items for when we executed our plan for her to leave town."

That explained the stash. In my mind, a thin thread connected that image to Anne.

"But we figured we'd have to explain this kind of stuff

to the cops when we left, because we were so sure that Royson would basically call 911 when Cress left."

"So what did you do?"

"We bought a pair of matching necklaces," Anne said. "One for me, and one for Cress. And then we had the jeweler drill a hole through the middle of Cress's necklace. My boyfriend is great with tech stuff, and he had this pinhole camera that he'd bought online, and he installed it in the necklace. And Cress wore that every day for like a week with her dad around so she could record how he was acting and basically all her conversations."

"Wow, okay," I said. "That's impressive. Good plan."

"Yeah, it was. But her dad got suspicious, so we decided to swap necklaces for a little while. Just until the heat was off. And then I buried the necklace out here. Cress was going to come fetch on the night she did the recording but... Yeah, you know what happened before she could get to it."

"Wag 'n bietjie," Hentie said. "Wait. So, which necklace was Cressida wearing on the night she died?"

"My necklace. The one without the camera," she said. "The killer took it. And I believe that Royson is the killer. He realized what we were doing, and decided to get rid of Cress once and for all." Tears streaked down Anne's cheeks. "He's awful. I can't believe that he did this, and I had to wait to come out here and get the evidence, so I can make sure that he pays for what he's done."

"This camera has an onboard chip?" I asked.

"Yeah, it's slotted into the back of the wire work surrounding the stone," she said. "It's an SD card. You can plug it into a phone."

Excitement swelled in my chest. "Seriously?"

"Yeah. I was going to take it to the police once I dug it up. I expected Royson to show up and try to stop me. That's kind of why I freaked out back there."

"I totally get that," I said. "I would have freaked out too."

"So, what do you think I should do?"

"Well, I think we should review the footage and see if there are any clues that prove Royson was the one planning to kill Cressida."

Anne hesitated. "Okay. We can do that."

"But tell me, Anne, when did you swap necklaces?" I asked.

"Like a day before she died," Anne said. "She had this fight with her dad, and he kept looking at the necklace funny so we decided to swap necklaces for a while in case he tried to confiscate it."

"Did he get physical with Cressida?" I asked.

"No," Anne said. "It wasn't like that. It was more about controlling everything that she did. He wanted money. He wanted her to work for him so that he could have her money, and he bought a house with it, and every-thing. What Cress wanted didn't matter."

"Got it," I said. "Look, let's head back to town. You can come to the Oceanside Guesthouse with us, and we'll review the footage together. That way, you'll be safe, and we can contact the cops from there. What do you say?"

Tears spilled onto Anne's cheeks, and she hugged Barkington, who hopped his paws up on her chest and licked her chin. "I'm so grateful for your help," she said. "I've been so afraid and alone. I've been missing work and messing up because I don't know how to handle this."

"You're a good person, Anne," I said. "And if you talk to Cookie about what's happened, I'm certain she'll take you back as an employee."

"Thanks," Anne said.

And then we helped her up and headed back through the cemetery toward the exit. We were so close to the truth, I could almost taste it.

# Twenty-Four

I WASN'T IN A RUSH TO REVIEW THE FOOTAGE right away, simply because Anne was shaky and needed help. And the footage wasn't going anywhere. We had it with us in the form of the necklace. On the ride back to the guesthouse, Hentie quizzed Anne while I focused on the road, trying not to let my thoughts overwhelm me.

Royson and Macy. Those were the suspects, but Anne was convinced that it was Royson who'd killed his daughter, and after Mama's warning, it was difficult not to draw the same conclusion.

*But the evidence has to back it up.*

I parked the ice cream truck outside the Oceanside, and we went in as a group, Barkington in Anne's arms, and Hentie leading the way, walking with her head held high. No eye twitches tonight.

Inside, we found Sam at the front desk, reading.

"There you are," she said. "I was just about to lock up for the evening. Oh, Anne, how nice to see you."

"Hi Sam," Anne said, with a small smile. "Do you mind if I use your bathroom?"

"Go ahead." Sam pointed down the hall.

Anne walked off, and Sam looked up at us, leaning in. "And? What's going on?"

"She might have answers about what happened to Cressida," I said. "Do you mind if she stays the night? I think she's pretty shaken up and doesn't want to go back to her place. I'll pay extra."

"No problem, April," Sam said. "And don't worry about paying extra. This is an extreme circumstance. She's so pale. Like she's seen a ghost."

I grimaced.

Hentie and I headed toward the dining area, which was already bustling with chatter and overflowing with the mouthwatering scents of whatever Shawn had decided to prepare for the evening.

"Hey, April, wait a second, will you?" Sam called.

I backed up, and Trouble darted around the side of the reception desk and batted my ankles. I smiled at the calico and bent to stroke him, but he was already off to go harass the rest of the guests, his tail stiff and jaunty.

"What's up?" I asked.

Sam stood up and tucked her hands into the front pocket of her apron. "Two things," she said. "Someone called earlier asking after you."

"Oh?" I played it cool, even though the skin on the back of my neck tingled. "Did they leave a name?"

"No name," she said. "But it was a guy with a... Well, I don't want to sound strange, but he had a very nice voice. Not too deep, kind of smooth and—" Sam laughed and blushed. "Anyway, he hung up when I said you weren't around. And then later, a handsome guy stopped by the guesthouse asking after you again. I think it was the same guy."

"Did he? That's not usually what happens to me." I forced a laugh.

*I have to get a phone and call Grant.*

But if I did that, he would find out I was compromised and this little trip would be over. The murder investigation, my friendship with Hentie, my time with Barkington, gone in the blink of an eye.

I kept my focus on my breathing. "Did he give you a name?"

"No," Sam said. "He said he would stop by again in the morning."

"Oh, that's weird," I said nonchalantly. "What did he look like?"

"Uh, handsome." Another coloring of the cheeks. "He

had dark hair and eyes, and he was wearing an expensive suit."

One of the men who had stopped to talk to Hentie?

"Thanks for letting me know," I said, as Anne reappeared in the hall with Barkington. She wore the necklace and touched her fingers to the stone, her eyes red-rimmed.

I guided Anne through to the dining area, and we took our seats at the table beside the front windows. Barkington sat in Anne's lap, and she covered the necklace with one hand. "Are you sure it's safe here?" she asked. "What if Royson finds us?"

"It's safe," I said. "I can promise you that much." I had taken the seat closest to the window with a view of the moonlight sparkling on the truck and the giant ice cream on top. "And besides that, we won't let anything happen to you. If you're right about the necklace, then we're about to find out the truth, and we can take that to Detective White." And by "we" I meant her. Because I couldn't risk turning up in a newspaper article in this small town.

Special Agent in Charge Grant would have kittens if that happened.

Sam and Shawn brought out drinks according to order, and we were treated to seafood pizza this evening. Anne ate like a woman possessed while I picked at my food.

Something was wrong, but I couldn't place my finger on it.

That foggy picture in my mind hadn't cleared. The corkboard didn't make sense, but the evidence pointed in one direction. Then why was I still concerned about this?

The necklace was the answer.

*And the second necklace.* If we could find that, it would be indisputable evidence of wrongdoing. Had Royson taken it from his daughter's neck?

"Anne," I said, after a bite of pizza. "Did you tell anyone about the camera other than Cory?"

"No," she said. "I didn't. I'm not sure about Cress, but I don't think she'd do that. She would have no reason to."

"Got it."

The rest of the dinner passed in a pleasant silence punctuated by occasional conversation, and slowly, Anne began to relax. The color returned to her cheeks. Barkington and Trouble played, darting around the dining room and out into the entry hall, and my gaze wandered to the truck outside.

And the dark figure standing beside it.

It was him.

It had to be.

And that meant I could deal with this problem quickly and effectively. I wouldn't have to tell Special Agent in

Charge Grant a darn thing if I got rid of this guy before he became an issue.

I excused myself from the table and walked down the hallway to my room. I unlocked it and entered. I grabbed my stun pen—a silver cylinder filled with fluid and ending in a viciously sharp needle—and opened the window. The fluid inside the pen would immobilize an attacker's muscles without hindering their ability to talk. Perfect for questioning another spy.

I climbed out of the window and walked down the side of the inn, scanning my surroundings.

The figure was still next to the truck, but around the front now, and they were peering through the windows.

I sneaked up behind them, ensuring I was out of sight of the front windows of the inn, then tapped the back of my stun pen to eject the needle. I brought the pen up and stabbed toward the guy's exposed neck, but he turned and caught my wrist.

"Don't," he said, and boy, Sam had been right. This guy was stunningly handsome.

Strong jawline, dark eyes, and clean shaven. He was much taller than me. And he wasn't one of the guys who had stopped next to the truck earlier.

I spun out of his grip and attacked again, leaping forward to inject him.

He dodged back. Good reflexes. Definitely a spy. "Stop."

I ignored him, spinning low and sweeping his leg. He tripped forward, and nearly fell, but side-stepped before I could inject his leg. It didn't matter where I got him with the needle, I just had to—

"Delta, stop."

Nobody knew my real name. Except my family and the NSIB.

I backed up, sheathing the pen. "Who are you?"

*Twenty-Five*

"MY NAME IS AGENT BRIAN SMULDER," HE SAID. "And I need to talk to you in private." He opened his jacket and flashed me his badge.

"I'm going to need to see that up close."

He removed it and handed it over to me, and I studied it. He was NSIB, or so the badge claimed, but I wasn't about to let him in because he claimed to be a part of my organization. I couldn't be sure that he was being truthful.

"Your Uncle sent me," Brian said. "Seriously. We need to talk indoors, in private."

"Fine. But if you try anything, I will kill you."

He nodded.

I handed him the badge then led the way around the side of the Oceanside to my window. I climbed in. Brian followed me, landing gracefully inside the room and turning to shut the window.

"You sure this room isn't bugged?" he asked, scanning the space.

And, shamefully, he was even more attractive in the light.

"I'm sure," I said. "I check it every day when I get back home."

"You checked it today?"

I glared at him. "Have at it, Smulder."

He moved through the room, searching the place for any sign of a bug or disturbance, and came back empty-handed. I checked the hall while he was busy, ensuring that nobody was listening in on our conversation, then put my pen back in my fanny pack on the dressing table.

Brian crossed his arms, the sleeves of his jacket stretching over his biceps. "Grant sent me," he said. "And, uh, this isn't the first time I've been on babysitting duty."

"What do you mean?" I asked.

"You didn't answer my calls," he said. "If you had, you would know what's going on."

"You know as well as I do that that phone was my line of contact with Grant. Not anyone else. No one was meant to have that number. And Grant didn't call me to tell me about you, which makes this entire scenario highly suspicious."

"He didn't have the chance," Smulder said. "I didn't even have the chance to pack my bags before they shipped me out here." There was resentment in his tone. "Grant's dealing with the fall-out of your mistake, and now I'm here to make sure you play by the rules."

"Suit and all?"

"I'll be changing as soon as I receive my cover," he said. "Which will be shortly, once I'm settled into a room at this guesthouse."

"Oh no. Absolutely not," I said. "I don't need you here."

"It doesn't matter what you need, or what you think you need, Mission," he growled.

"Waters," I said. "Seriously? Grant sent you? And you don't even know my cover name?"

"I do," he breathed, then ruffled that dark hair with a tan hand. "I've had the pleasure of working with your family before."

That took me by surprise. "What? Georgina?" I whispered.

"No."

"Charlie?"

His jaw tightened and clenched. "Yes."

*Touched a nerve.* Looked like Charlie and Mr. Smulder had been more than friends. "Ah. She's fun," I said. "I bet you had a blast."

"Not really." He inhaled through his nose. "Moving on," he said. "I'm going to be looking out for you. Consider me your safety net."

I exhaled.

Great. Another obstacle to navigate. "Look, Brian, you seem like a nice enough guy, but I don't need a safety net. I haven't messed up that badly that I need you here. It's not like my cover has been outed."

"You've got a friend," he said. "That's Grant's concern. He doesn't want you to kick her off your truck yet, but I'll be watching." He took a step toward me, his shoes tapping on the boards. "And I'll be here to help if you need me."

*Well, excuse me.* I cleared my throat and broke eye contact with him.

"Grant's had some bad experiences with your family," Smulder said. "So, uh, yeah, I think he's covering his bases by sending me here."

I nodded slowly. "Right, sure."

"Look, I'm not going to make your life difficult. That's not my goal. But I am the kind of guy who does his job and does it well." It was a warning.

"We have that in common," I said. "One mistake doesn't make me bad at my job, if that's what you're insinuating."

"It's not. April—"

A knock rattled the door and was followed by a bark

from Barkington. "April?" Hentie called. "April, is jy okay? Agh. I mean, are you okay?" Another knock.

"You have to go," I whispered, pointing to the window.

Brian gave me one last look—a warning—and then opened the window and clambered out. He closed it behind himself.

"Coming." I walked to the door and opened it for Hentie.

Barkington dashed inside, Hentie and Anne followed, though Hentie stopped after a few steps. "Smells like man in here."

"What?" Both Anne and I asked.

"You know, cologne. Man perfume. It's nice."

"Uh, you must be mistaken," I said, and opened the window. "But here's some fresh air. Maybe Shawn was in here earlier to clean."

Anne sat down in an armchair and removed the necklace. She handed it to me, and I turned it over and fiddled with the wiring that held it in place. The SD card wasn't hard to remove, thankfully, and I inserted it into Hentie's phone.

The three of us gathered around, Hentie sitting on the sofa, scooched right to the edge, and me kneeling in front of the coffee table.

"The file isn't very large," I said, and hit the button to play the video on the device.

An image appeared of the cemetery, not at night, but during the day, and I turned up the sound.

"This must be when Cress and Macy were scouting out the cemetery," Anne said. "They mentioned they were going to do that the day before the recording."

Cressida walked along, the view from the necklace showing off the cemetery during the day time, the trees and grass green, the stones glistening with morning dew.

"This is going to be great," Cressida said. "I'm super excited to do this, Macy. I'm so glad you could be a part of this."

"Yeah, me too," Macy replied. "I can't thank you enough for inviting me to collab."

"It's nothing," she said. "Honestly, I hate to say it but I'm mostly doing it to annoy my dad. He doesn't like the idea of 'handouts' and that's what he thinks us working together is."

"You're kidding," Macy said. "Is this about... You know."

"What, me not believing in ghosts?" Cressida asked, and it was haunting to hear her voice now that she had died.

"Yeah."

"No," Cressida said. "I mean, if it was up to me, I

wouldn't even have this channel." She turned to face Macy, and we caught a glimpse of her face, her hair long and dank and hanging loose.

"Can I tell you a secret?" Cressida whispered. "This necklace I'm wearing?"

"Yeah?" Macy leaned in, peering at it.

"It's not even cursed. I got it from a jeweler. And it's got a camera inside it. It's literally recording everything. That way, when I leave, my father won't be able to hunt me down because I'll have evidence of everything he's done."

"Like what, Cress?" Macy's face filled with concern. "What could he—?"

The recording cut off.

Hentie and Anne started talking but I didn't take in a word of it.

I rose and walked to the window, unseeing, as the foggy image in my mind cleared.

It was an image of Royson, Cressida, and Macy, standing in front of the cemetery before they'd gone inside on the night of Cressida's murder. And Macy was staring at her. Not at her, but at the necklace around her throat.

The necklace she thought held the camera. And there was a sneer on her face.

Macy's hair was loose, and she wore a hoodie in the

image. But on the night I'd run into her, her hair had been tied back, and there had been no hoodie in sight.

"Anne," I said, turning to face the women. "Do you know where Macy lives?"

"Uh, yeah. She lives on Berry Lane. Literally a few houses down from me. Why?" Anne asked.

"Well, we'll probably need to talk to her about all of this. Maybe we can ask her about the rest of the conversation." But that wasn't the real reason I wanted her address.

"I can't believe it," Anne said. "There's nothing on here." She slumped in the armchair, clutching her forehead.

"Don't give up hope, poppie," Hentie said, and patted her arm. "It will be okay. Come on. Let's get some rest. You can sleep in my room. Sam said she would bring in an extra mattress for you." The pair rose and said goodnight. I patted Barkington on the head, then closed the door behind them.

I changed into all black clothing, opened the window, and climbed out into the night.

# Twenty-Six

THE PUZZLE PIECES CLICKED INTO PLACE AS I walked down the sidewalk, heading toward Berry Lane. Macy's channel had taken off. She had thought Cressida hadn't deserved the fame because she didn't believe in ghosts, and she had recorded and threatened Royson.

She had used the tragedy in her favor. Used it to launch her ViewTube channel. Her motive was fame. Money. Success.

She had been jealous of Cressida.

A footstep crunched behind me, and I stopped and turned, scanning the empty street, the bushes and trees in quaint front yards.

"Come out," I said.

Nothing.

"Smulder."

He stepped out from behind a tree, wearing a sheepish grin. He'd changed into a pair of jeans and a black t-shirt that sat snug against his frame.

"Seriously?" I asked. "You're following me."

"That's my job," he said. "I told you. Safety net."

"I'm surprised you're not telling me I have to stop and go home."

"I should," he said, then shrugged. "But I'm curious to see how this pans out."

I frowned at him and adjusted my fanny pack. I wasn't sure what I'd need to use to bring down justice on Macy's head, but I had everything I needed, and Brian Smulder wasn't part of my toolkit.

"Go back to the guesthouse, Brian."

"You can call me Oliver," he said.

I sighed. "Fine. Go back to the guesthouse, Oliver. I've got things to do." I walked off, rolling my eyes at the sound of him following me.

Finally, I passed Anne's house and continued past the rows of cute houses with picket fences until I reached Macy's place. It was a small square house across from a grassy patch that was the local park. Her curtains were open, affording a view of the kitchen and living room. The front door was a shade of peach. The trash cans at the side of the house drew my eye.

I moved toward them, but laughter from the kitchen made me duck down.

Macy paced back and forth inside, talking on the phone. "I know, right? I'm going to be so friggin' rich! And that Royson has no idea what to do with himself. His channel is falling apart. Yeah, of course, I'm sad about Cressida. That's so awful, but the point is, I'm doing great, Mom. Like, amazing. Aw, thanks. I knew you'd be proud of me."

I cringed inwardly and crouched down, hurrying along the side of the house. A girl like Macy, arrogant, full of herself, wouldn't go to much effort to dispose of those clothes. She thought she was in the clear. She'd been entirely unconcerned by the police investigations because she believed that she had what she needed. The necklace with the camera.

"I already have my next video planned, by the way." She wore a small smile. "Yeah, I found this necklace in the Mary McClary house. I'm going to do a video on it."

*She's some special kind of dumb.*

I moved to the trash can, snapping on a pair of latex gloves. Carefully, I lifted the lid and found sealed plastic bags waiting.

"This is how you like to spend evenings?" Brian whispered, close behind me.

I removed a knife from my fanny pack and tore into

the trash. The first bag was full of orange peels and plastic wrappers. I moved it down in the trash can and brought another bag up from the bottom, tore into that one next. Nothing.

"She's going to hear all that noise," Brian murmured.

"Then keep an eye on her, *Oliver*," I hissed.

"I should drag you out of here."

"I'd like to see you try. I'm still carrying that shock pen."

"See if you can stick me with it this time," he replied.

I held back my frustration. Now wasn't the time to let a man get under my skin, even if he was a handsome one. Not that I cared. I'd already loved and lost. I wasn't interested in romance, especially not with another agent. That spelled complications.

I fished around at the bottom of the trash can and found a squashed plastic bag. I heaved it up and the trash can slid to the side. I braced myself for the noise, but Smulder caught it before it hit the ground. He placed it down flat.

"Thanks," I whispered.

"Don't mention it," he said. "Seriously, do *not* mention it."

I chuckled under my breath, then pierced the final bag. I opened it up and sucked in a breath. "Got her," I murmured.

I'd found the bloodied hoodie she'd been wearing on that night. And she had the necklace on her throat right now.

I left the hoodie where it was, then placed the lid back on top of the trash can.

"What are you doing?" Brian whispered. "Not going to go in there and take her down?"

"What would that achieve?" I asked. "I need the cops to arrest her. And I need to be far away from here when they do. Help me pull this trash can out to the sidewalk, will you?"

We carried it out together, carefully lifting it over the picket fence, and placing it on the sidewalk where the cops would be able to search it, legally, without a warrant.

"Got a phone?"

Brian frowned at me.

"Please?"

Brian removed a cellphone from his pocket. I stripped off the gloves as I crossed the street, stopping only to dispose of them in a trash can in the park.

I sat down on a wrought iron bench. Brian took a spot beside me and handed me his phone.

I called in the tip about the hoodie to 911 then hung up and sat back to enjoy the show.

Ten minutes later, two police cruisers pulled up outside the house. Detective White got out of the first and immediately started searching the trash while we watched from the shadows under an old oak tree.

It wouldn't take long for a judge to approve a warrant for Macy's arrest.

This case was closed.

# Twenty-Seven

*One week later...*

"I heard that Royson's leaving town in disgrace," Hentie said. "Apparently, his ViewTube channel got shut down. Serves him right after everything he did to his daughter. His mother is going to live with relatives as well."

"Where did you hear that?" I asked, as I took a bite of my stack of fluffy pancakes. It was a beautiful summer's morning at the Oceanside, and the window was open to let in the salty ocean breeze. The ice cream truck sparkled in the sunlight outside—we'd taken it to a car wash yesterday.

"Anne told me," Hentie said. "She's working at the

bakery again, remember? We got those cupcakes yesterday?"

"Right, of course." I'd been distracted over the last week. Not because of any murder cases. Macy had been arrested shortly after Detective White had gone through her trash and found the evidence.

No, I was distracted because of the new addition to the Oceanside.

Brian Smulder had become my unofficial shadow. It was a miracle that Hentie hadn't noticed.

"I'm just glad everything is working out for the best," Hentie continued, as she fed Barkington a wedge of cheese from her plate. He gobbled it up and licked her fingers. "I've been having an amazing time on the truck, April. I don't want it to end any time soon."

"Me neither," I said. "I—" But I cut off as Brian entered the room.

His wavy hair was parted to one side, and he wore a white t-shirt and a pair of blue jeans that were faded. I swallowed and looked away.

"There he is," Hentie whispered, tapping my arm.

"Huh?"

"The guy you obviously have a crush on," Hentie said.

"No idea what you mean." I stared out of the front window, stubbornly. I didn't like Brian. In fact, I wished

Brian would leave Carmel Springs and never come back. Because Brian was officially cramping my style.

He was everywhere I looked.

"If it makes you feel any better," Hentie said, "I think he likes you too. He stares at you every time we have dinner or breakfast."

"Stop, Hentie. It's not like that. And I'm not interested in dating. I just— I lost someone close to me."

Hentie squeezed my hand. "I'm so sorry, April. I didn't know."

"That's okay," I said, and smiled at her. "Let's just talk about something else. We've got big plans for the coming week. I really want us to push the Caramel Drip because I feel like it's not selling as well as the other flavors. We could top it with bits of fudge and that might work. What do you think?"

"Wonderlik! I love that idea." Hentie clapped her hands.

I glanced to the left and found Brian eyeing me from his table near the kitchen doors. He made eyes at me, gesturing to his phone. A notification blipped in my pocket, and I squeezed my phone out and unlocked the screen.

OLIVER

I checked out those guys you told me about.

> Yeah?

> They were just businessmen passing through. Nothing in their backgrounds to be alarmed about.

> Thanks.

> That's what I'm here for.

A job. He was here for a job, and I was here to try to keep my cover. I hated this. I hated that Brian was here because he was a constant reminder of the fact that this was all fake, and that I had started to like my time on the ice cream truck.

This was crazy. It had been a couple of weeks, and I'd made a friend I enjoyed spending time with, and met amazing people. I didn't want to move on from this yet.

The front doors of the guesthouse banged, and the noise of suitcases rolling into the inn's foyer followed.

A scream rang out.

Both Hentie and I craned our necks to get a glimpse of what was causing the commotion.

Sam stood in front of the reception desk, squealing and clapping her hands. Two women had entered the inn, one of them was tall, with poker-straight gray hair. The other was shorter, middle-aged, and with short brown locks that framed a heart-shaped face.

"I can't believe you're here," Sam squealed, and drew both of them into a hug.

"Easy, Sam," the gray-haired woman said. "You're choking me before lunch. And Ruby made me wake up at the crack of dawn to get out here."

Sam stepped back, laughing, and patted the older woman on her arm. "Oh, Bee, you're such a card."

"We had to come pay you a visit before I got too big," the brunette said, stroking a hand over her stomach.

"I'm so happy you came," Sam said, "What can I get you? Are you hungry?"

Bee flashed a smile that showed off a gap between her two front teeth. "Anything with a high sugar content will suit me just fine."

And then the three of them bustled into the dining area. Ruby and Bee took two steps inside before their gazes fell on us.

A frown wrinkled Bee's forehead. "Huh. They're in our spot."

"Your spot?" Hentie asked.

"Sorry," Ruby said, with a musical laugh. "She just means that, well, when we used to live here, we always sat at that table. That's all. It's totally fine. We'll find somewhere else to sit."

But Bee didn't seem impressed.

"You're more than welcome to join us," I said.

"Seriously?" Ruby asked.

"Ja." Hentie grinned at them, and Barkington gave a few yaps of approval.

"Oh this is perfect," Sam said, clapping her hands again. "You guys are going to get on like a house on fire."

Bee's hazel eyes were bright as she scanned us both. "We'll see about that," she said.

✇

*What shenanigans will Delta and Hentie get up to next in Carmel Springs, Maine? Will Delta and Smulder learn to get along? And how will Delta handle the arrival of the infamous sleuthing duo that is Ruby and Bee? Find out in CARAMEL DRIP MURDER.*

Craving More Cozy Mystery?

**If you had fun with Delta Mission, you'll, love getting to know Charlie Mission and her butt-kicking grandmother, Georgina. You can read the first chapter of Charlie's story, *The Case of the Waffling Warrants*, below!**

"Come in, Big G, come in." I spoke under my breath so that the flesh-colored microphone seated against my throat picked up my voice. "What is your status?"

My grandmother, Georgina—pet name Gamma, code name Big G—was out on a special operation. Reconnaissance at the newest guesthouse in our town, Gossip. The reason? First, she was an ex-spy, as was I, and second, the woman who'd opened the guesthouse was her mortal enemy and in direct competition with my grandmother's establishment, the Gossip Inn.

Who was this enemy, this bringer of potential financial doom?

A middle-aged woman with a penchant for wearing pashminas and annoying anyone who looked her way.

Jessie Belle-Blue.

It was rumored that even thinking the woman's name summoned a murder of crows.

"I repeat, Big G, what is your status?"

"I'm en route to the nest," my grandmother replied in my earpiece.

I let out a relieved sigh and exited my bedroom, heading downstairs to help with the breakfast service.

In the nine months since I had retired as a spy, life in Gossip had been normal. In the Gossip sense of the term. I'd expected that my job as a server, maid, and assistant would bring the usual level of "cat herding" inherent when working at the inn. Whether that involved tracking down runaway cats, literally, or providing a guest with a moist towelette after a fainting spell—tempers ran high in Gossip.

What was the reason for the craziness? Shoot, it had to be something in the water.

I took the main stairs two at a time and found my friend, the inn's chef, paging through her recipe book in the lime green kitchen. Lauren Harris wore her red hair in a French braid today, apron stretched over her pregnant belly.

"Morning," I said, "how are you today?"

"Madder than a fat cat on a diet." She slapped her recipe book closed and turned to me.

*Uh oh. Looks like it's time for more cat herding.*

"What's wrong?"

"My supplier is out of flour and sugar. Can you believe that?" Lauren huffed, smoothing her hands over her belly while the clock on the wall ticked away. Breakfast was in two hours and Lauren loved baking cupcakes as part of the meal.

"Do you have enough supplies to make cupcakes for this morning?"

"Yes. But just for today," Lauren replied. "The guests are going to love my new waffle cupcakes, and they'll be sore they can't get anymore after this batch is done. Why, I should go down there and wring Billy's neck for doing this to me. He knows I take an order of sugar and flour every week, and I get it at just above cost too. What's Georgina going to say?"

"Don't stress, Lauren," I said. "We'll figure it out."

"Right." She brightened a little. "I nearly forgot you're the one who "fixes" things around here." Lauren winked at me.

She was the only person in the entire town who knew that my grandmother and I had once been spies for the NSIB—the National Security Investigative Bureau. But the news that I had helped solve several murders had spread through town, and now, anybody and everybody with a problem would call me up asking for help. A lot of them offered me money. And I was selective about who I chose to help.

"I'll check it out for you if you'd like," I said. "The flour issue."

"Nah, that's OK. I'm sure Billy will get more stock this week. I'll lean on him until he squeals."

"Sounds like you've been picking up tips from Georgina."

Lauren giggled then returned to her super-secret recipe book—no one but she was allowed to touch it.

"What's on the menu this morning?" I asked.

Lauren was the boss in the kitchen—she told me what to do, and I followed her instructions precisely. If I did anything else, like trying to read the recipe for instance, the food would end up burned, missing ingredients or worse.

The only place I wasn't a "fixer" was in the Gossip Inn's kitchen.

"Bacon and eggs over easy, biscuits and gravy, waffle cupcakes and... oh, I can't make fresh baked bread, can I?"

"Tell her I'll bring some back with me from the

bakery." Gamma's voice startled me. Goodness, I'd forgotten about the earpiece—she could hear everything happening in the kitchen.

"I'll text Georgina and ask her to bring bread from the bakery."

"You're a lifesaver, Charlotte."

We set to work on the breakfast—it was 7:00 a.m. and we needed everything done within two hours—and fell into our easy rhythm of baking and cooking.

My grandmother entered the kitchen at around 8:30 a.m., dressed in a neat silk blouse and a pair of slacks rather than the black outfit she'd left in for her spy mission. Tall, willowy, and with neatly styled gray hair, Gamma had always reminded me of Helen Mirren playing the Queen.

"Good morning, ladies," she said, in her prim, British accent. "I bring bread and tidings."

"What did you find out?" I asked.

"No evidence of the supposed ghost tours," Gamma said.

We'd started hosting ghost tours at the inn recently, so of course Jessie Belle-Blue wanted to do the same. She was all about under-cutting us, but, thankfully, the Gossip Inn had a legacy and over 1,000 positive reviews on Trip-Advisor.

Breakfast time arrived, and the guests filled the quaint dining area with its glossy tables, creaking wooden floors, and egg yolk yellow walls. Chatter and laughter leaked through the swinging kitchen doors with their porthole windows.

"That's my cue," I said, dusting off my apron, and heading out into the dining room.

I picked up a pot of coffee from the sideboard where we kept the drinks station and started my rounds.

Most of the guests had gathered around a center table in the dining room, and bursts of laughter came from the group, accompanied by the occasional shout.

I elbowed my way past a couple of guests—nobody could accuse me of having great people skills—apologizing along the way until I reached the table. The last time something like this had happened, a murder had followed shortly afterward.

*Not this time. No way.*

"—the last thing she'd ever hear!" The woman seated at the table, drawing the attention, was vaguely familiar. She wore her dark hair in luscious curls, and tossed it as she spoke, looking down her upturned nose at the people around the table.

"What happened then, Mandy?" Another woman asked, her hands clasped together in front of her stomach.

*Mandy? Wait a second, isn't this Mandy Gilmore?*

Gamma had mentioned her once before—Mandy was

a massive gossip in town. Why wasn't she staying at her house?

"What happened? Well, she ran off with her tail between her legs, of course. She'll soon learn not to cross me. Heaven knows, I always repay my debts."

"What, like a Lannister from *Game of Thrones*?" That had come from a taller woman with ginger curls.

"Shut up, Opal," Mandy replied. "You have no idea what we're talking about, and even if you did, you wouldn't have the intelligence to comprehend it."

The crowd let out various 'oofs' in response to that. The woman next to me clapped her hand over her mouth.

"You're all talk, Gilmore." Opal lifted a hand and yammered it at the other woman. "You act like you're a threat, but we know the truth around here."

"The truth?" Mandy leaned in, pressing her hands flat onto the tabletop, the crystal vase in the center rattling. "And what's that, Opal, darling? I'd love to hear it."

"That you're a failure. You sold your house, left Gossip with your head in the clouds, told everyone you were going to become a successful businesswoman, and now you're back. Back to scrape together the pieces of the life you have left."

"Witch!" Mandy scraped her chair back.

"All right, all right," I said, setting down the coffee pot

on the table. "That's enough, ladies. Everyone head back to their tables before things get out of hand."

Both Opal and Mandy stared daggers at me.

I flashed them both smiles. "We wouldn't want to ruin breakfast, would we? Lauren's prepared waffle cupcakes."

That distracted them. "Waffle cupcakes?" Opal's brow wrinkled. "How's that going to work?"

"Let's talk about it at your table." I grabbed my coffee pot and walked her away from Mandy. The crowd slowly dispersed, people muttering regret at having missed out on a show. The Gossip Inn was popular for its constant conflict.

If the rumors didn't start here then they weren't worth repeating. That was the mantra, anyway.

I seated Opal at her table, and she pursed her lips at me. "You shouldn't have interrupted. That woman needs a piece of my mind."

"We prefer peace of mind at the inn." I put up another of my best smiles.

Compared to what I'd been through in the past— hiding out from my rogue spy ex-husband and eventually helping put him behind bars when he found me—dealing with the guests was a cakewalk.

"What brings you to Gossip, Opal?" I asked.

"I live here," she replied, waspishly. "I'm staying here while they're fumigating my house. Roaches."

"Ah." I struggled not to grimace. Thankfully, my cell phone buzzed in the front pocket of my apron and distracted me. "Coffee?"

"I don't take caffeine." And she said it like I'd offered her an illegal substance too.

"Call me if you need anything." I hurried off before she could make good on that promise, bringing my phone out of my pocket.

I left the coffee pot on the sideboard, moving into the Gossip Inn's spacious foyer, the chandelier overhead off, but catching light in glimmers. The tables lining the hall were filled with trinkets from the days when the inn had been a museum—an eclectic collection of bits and bobs.

"This is Charlotte Smith," I answered the call—I would never get to use my true last name, Mission, again, but it was safer this way.

"Hello, Charlotte." A soft, rasping voice. "I've been trying to get through to you. I'm desperate."

"Who is this?"

"My name is Tina Rogers, and I need your help."

"My help."

"Yes," she said. "I understand that you have a certain set of skills. That you fix people's problems?"

"I do. But it depends on the problem and the price." I didn't have a set fee for helping people, but if it drew me away from the inn for long, I had to charge. I was technically a consultant now. Sort of like a P.I. without the fedora and coffee-stained shirt.

"My mother will handle your fee," Tina said. "I've asked her to text you about it, but I... I don't have long to talk. They're going to pull me off the phone soon."

"Who?"

"The police," she replied. "I'm calling you from the holding cell at the Gossip Police Station. I've been arrested on false charges, and I need you to help me prove my innocence."

"Miss Rogers, it's probably a better idea to invest in a lawyer." But I was tempted. It had been a long time since I'd felt useful.

"No! I'm not going to a lawyer. I'm going to make these idiots pay for ever having arrested me."

I took a breath. "OK. Before I accept your... case, I'll need to know what happened. You'll need to tell me every-thing." I glanced through the open doorway that led into the dining room. No one looked unhappy about the lack of service yet.

"I can't tell you everything now. I don't have much time."

"So give me the *CliffsNotes*."

"I was arrested for breaking into and vandalizing Josie Carlson's bakery, The Little Cake Shop. Apparently, they found my glove there—it was specially embroidered, you see—but it's not mine because—" The line went dead.

"Hello? Miss Rogers?" I pulled the cellphone away from my ear and frowned at the screen. "Darn."

My interest was piqued. A mystery case about a break-in that involved the local bakery? Which just so happened to be run by one of my least favorite people in Gossip?

And when I'd just started getting bored with the push and pull of everyday life at the inn?

*Count me in.*

Want to read more? You can grab **the first book** in *the Gossip Cozy Mystery series* on all major retailers.

Happy reading, friend!